W9-CUB-913

# DOG IN THE DARK

By the same author:

# DOG
## IN THE
# DARK

## Gerald Hammond

St. Martin's Press
New York

Library of Congress Cataloging-in-Publication Data

Hammond, Gerald.
      Dog in the dark.

      I. Title.
PR6058.A55456D6  1990          823'.914          89-24226
ISBN 0-312-03819-4

First published in Great Britain by Macmillan London Limited.

First U.S. Edition

10 9 8 7 6 5 4 3 2 1

## Author's Note

Once, when writing an article about gundogs, I rashly changed the name of an offender in order not to embarrass its owner. The result, of course, was an indignant lady complaining to the magazine, and to anybody else who would pay attention, that it was certainly not her Bonzo (or whatever the name was) who chased the hare or crunched the pheasant. The details are vague by now but the scars remain.

So let me state that, just as the human characters are fictitious, if any of the canines represented here have ever had real-life counterparts these have belonged to myself or my family. Even so, the resemblances are mostly in name. Let's say rather that many of the dogs in this story are dogs I would have liked to own.

My own fancy is for Labradors, but Labs are too predictable for such a story as this. In turning over to spaniels, I leaned heavily on the writings of Peter (P. R. A.) Moxon. If my facts are correct, the credit is his. Any errors are all my own.

G. H.

# ONE

I glanced over my shoulder to make sure that I was not leaving the judges behind and at that moment the Gun to my right fired a shot.

The stewards with their red flags had allowed the spectators up close for once and a momentary recurrence of stagefright distracted me. When I looked forward again, the low sun was in my eyes. I could not pick up any falling bird against the moving branches and whirling leaves of the wood ahead. Had he missed, or taken a rabbit or a low bird? I had not heard the whirr of a rising pheasant but a stiff breeze was sighing among the dead leaves and in my ears as I turned. We were down to four dogs now. This was only a Novice Stake, but I was in a position to take Mistleton Moonbeam a step further on the long road to becoming a Field Trials Champion. Dear God, I told myself, don't let me blow it now!

'Get that bird from here,' said the nearer judge. He was Joe Little and I had run under him before – a fair judge but sometimes severe. I thought that he knew that I had missed the fall and was giving me a hint. Well, there was nothing for it but to hope that Moon had marked the bird.

The little spaniel had dropped at the sound of the shot. I gave her the signal to go out and she scampered forward, straight as a ruler. I began to breathe again. Short of the trees, she jinked to one side and checked at a patch of brambles. The bird, I decided, was a runner, but she was onto it.

Moon bobbed down and then started back towards me, but instead of the pheasant which I expected she was carrying a rabbit, plucked from its 'form' or 'seat'. There was a snicker of amusement from among the spectators.

My heart pounded. Disaster was very close. If I had to take it from her, we would be put out. I gave her the 'stop' whistle and when she squatted down I signalled her to 'drop it'. She paused and gave me one of her 'I hope you know what you're doing' looks but she released her hold. The rabbit nearly gave me heart failure by crouching for a few seconds as if injured but then bolted for the wood. Moon sat tight, watching it away in disgust. No penalty. There was even a thin spatter of applause.

I gave her a few seconds to forget about the rabbit and then sent her back to her original line. I could only see her head but she seemed to have picked up a scent. She put on a turn of speed and vanished into the wood.

There was nothing to do but wait. She could have scented another rabbit – they were almost as thick on the ground as the leaves in the air and she would have had the scent of rabbit fresh in her sensitive nose – but there are times when you can only trust the dog.

'It fell near the big clump of gorse,' the judge said at last.

I only nodded. Give her a little more time, I told myself. She had passed close downwind of that gorse. If a shot bird had been in there, even in that blustery wind, she would surely have scented it. But there was dead ground between the gorse and the trees. If I whistled and if the bird were a runner, I might be handling her away from it . . .

Her white markings showed through the undergrowth. She was coming back. She emerged into the open with a cock pheasant struggling in her jaws and returned to me at a gallop, her stump of a tail an almost invisible blur. She delivered the bird sitting – an unnecessary refinement but one which usually pleases the judges. Before wringing its neck, I held it up so that the judges could see that it was

8

alive – it has been known for an unscrupulous competitor to go through the motions of killing an already dead bird in order to distract the judges' attention from the damage inflicted by a hard-mouthed dog.

Joe Little checked between the feathers, looking for signs of shot. 'I think we've seen enough,' he said and the other judge nodded. They conferred.

Ten minutes later they announced their findings. Moonbeam was the outright winner. I was too elated to take in the other placings and the Certificates of Merit, but there would be time enough to read the details later in the sporting press. I thanked the host and his head keeper, went up to receive our award and then slipped away. Moonbeam danced all the way to the car. She knew that she had done well. Perhaps my mood had communicated itself and she certainly knew that her evening feed was due, but dogs develop an uncanny instinct for competition. She would have been much less boisterous if we had been unplaced.

There was a large hotel a few miles down the road. I pulled in, as much because I was exhausted and chilled through by the wind as to cadge some hot water for Moonbeam's dinner. It was a place of fake antiques and with oak beams stuck on as an afterthought, but it was warm. I ordered the lightest snack on the menu for myself and then carried Moon's dinner outside. When the kennel-meal had soaked up most of the water I fed her in the back of the car.

'You're a clever little bastard,' I told her. 'We'll try to get you an entry in an Open Stake next month, and if you do well in it we'll maybe find you a handsome husband and take a litter off you in the spring. You'll enjoy that,' I assured her. But she was intent on guzzling her dinner and responded only with a token wag of her docked tail. At other times, she gave me her full attention and all the loyalty in the world. I only wished that she could give me a little of her appetite.

My own snack was waiting for me in the bar. I carried

it to a corner table and settled down. There was soporific Muzak playing and I could easily have leaned back and fallen asleep. I never felt less like eating but I knew that only food would give me the energy to face the long drive home.

I was pushing the last of the food around my plate when a figure loomed between me and the lights of the bar. I looked up. Joe Little was standing over me. 'I thought I recognised your car outside,' he said. 'Do you mind if I join you?'

'You're welcome to,' I said. I was not feeling much like company just then, but to alienate a prominent judge would be about as advisable as insulting one's dentist.

He went back to the bar and returned with a laden tray, put down a substantial meal and a pint for himself and then pushed another pint in front of me. 'It is lager you're drinking?' he asked.

'It is.' I had reservations about drinking another pint on top of the half-pint I had had already, but I could probably leave some of it behind without being too obvious about it. 'Thank you. But I should be buying you the drinks.'

He laughed and shook his head. Amusement sat well on his square but kindly face. 'That would smack of corruption,' he said. 'And there's no need for any *quid pro quo*. That's a good little bitch you have there. If you do your part, she'll make Champion within another year, you mark my words. You earned the win, between you. Am I right in thinking that you already have a winner? Champion Mistleton Sunbeam,' he added, in case I had forgotten.

'That's right,' I said. 'Sunbeam and Moonbeam. They're full sisters. My sister-in-law named them.'

'One of my clients saw her in last year's Championship Stake. Very impressed, he was. If you're thinking of breeding from her, he wants you to put a dog pup aside for him and train it.'

'I thought you only went in for Labradors,' I said.

'Not so much of the "only",' he said with a snort of laughter.

'All right, I thought you specialised in Labradors.'

'You spaniel men think that when God had created the springer and its near relatives he should have knocked off for a dirty weekend.'

'I have always suspected that he did,' I said.

'And Labradors were the result.' Having scored a good point, Joe took a pull at his pint and beamed at me. 'Many a Labrador owner keeps a spaniel or two for the dirty work. What do you say?'

'Sunbeam's in pup now,' I told him.

'The sire?'

I told him and he whistled. 'I bet that cost you an arm and a leg,' he said.

'Not really. He has pick of the litter. Your client can have second choice if he confirms straight away.' I was waking up again, warmed by our talk. I finished my snack and began on the pint of lager.

'I'll tell him.' Joe was silent for a minute while he made some inroads into his steak and chips. 'Ever thought of turning fully professional?' he asked suddenly.

'Yes, of course I have,' I told him. 'Three or four people have been after me to train dogs for them.'

'Then why don't you?'

'There's no space for expansion where I am. I'm living with my brother and his wife. If I could find a suitable place within my means . . . '

Until then he had only been keeping the conversation going rather than letting it lapse into one of those awkward silences, but I saw his interest quicken. 'If you mean that,' he said, 'there's a place for sale near me. A farmhouse and barn with a few acres around them, not going at a giveaway price, but reasonable.'

I had heard such words rather often during the previous year, from friends. Frequently they had been used to describe an overpriced slum with inadequate ground space

11

and much dangerous traffic nearby. But Joe Little had his feet on the ground and he knew the world of dogs. I felt a stirring of cautious interest. 'There's reasonable and reasonable,' I said. 'It would have to be very reasonable to be anything other than a pipe-dream. I have a small pension and a little capital, but I'd have to build kennels and lay out some money on bitches. I don't know . . . '

'It's up to yourself,' he said, 'but I think you could make it.' He talked on, juggling figures in the air from his considerable experience – capital, turnover, profit. He made them sound very convincing, but my tired mind refused to take them in. 'One good thing about dogs, the generations come around quickly,' he went on. 'With people, you wait nearly twenty years; but if you keep the bitches from your first two litters you'll have a breeding stock from a very good line in a few years. Sooner, if you do a little trading.'

'You make it sound very easy,' I said. 'And in normal circumstances you'd probably be right. But I honestly don't think that I'd have the stamina to start something like that from scratch.'

He nodded sympathetically. 'I heard that you weren't keeping well. Amazing how good a grapevine the trials world has. But, in fact, it shows. You were in the army, weren't you? Stopped an Argy bullet in the Falklands?'

'No,' I said. 'As a matter of fact— '

He was not listening. 'But you've been walking around all day today. If you can walk, you can train. That's what you're good at. You enjoy the training side above anything else, or am I wrong?'

He seemed to have me weighed up. 'How do you know that?' I asked curiously.

'Instinct.' He stopped and thought about it. 'Your bitch works as though she was trained by somebody who had his heart in it. That's as well as I can put it. Let me tell you something.' He put aside his knife and fork and pointed at me. 'Never mind what anybody else tells you, if you can train, you can make a living, because that's where the money is. The puppy-factories have ruined the bottom end of the market but pups from winning strains always sell. Trained dogs sell better. How many Best English guns have you seen around?'

'Quite a few.'

'All right, so a good gun will last for ever. But how many Range Rovers do you see?' I opened my mouth to answer but he rushed on. 'Hundreds. A man's a fool if he'll pay that much for a car and grudge a tenth of the price for a good dog. He'll get a damned sight more pleasure out of the dog. And then there's always the other kind of a fool with a bank account who'll pay you to undo the mistakes he's made with his own dog. Get yourself a partner with a little capital, take on a kennel-maid for the rough work and you're in business. You might not make a mint, but you'd have a good life and a steady income.'

He made it sound a tempting alternative to continuing the abuse of my brother's hospitality and a life of comparative aimlessness but I could feel the old inertia creeping up on me. 'I'll think about it,' I said. And I knew that I would think about it, regretfully, cursing on my own lack of drive.

'You're tired,' he said. 'Why don't you come back with me now? Have a good night's sleep at my place and take a look at Three Oaks in the morning? Leave your car. I'm delivering a dog near here tomorrow, so I can bring you back again.'

I knew that Joe lived somewhere in Fife. It lay in the wrong direction, but after a tiring day the prospect of being driven the shorter distance by somebody else instead of tackling the long drive on my own was very tempting. If I phoned my brother, he would walk and feed Sunbeam for me. 'It's very kind of you—' I said doubtfully.

He tried to look indignant but his face was not made for it. 'I hate to see a young chap pottering around in an amateur way when he could be having a go,' he said. 'Especially an ex-officer. And if we're going to have a puppy explosion, I'd rather see dogs bred and trained by somebody who knows what he's doing instead of pups sired in the back garden by the dog next door and half-trained in the shooting field by incompetents. That's not kindness, it's my interfering nature.'

# TWO

Joe owned a modern house, well designed and lovingly furnished. Either there was money in the family or a breeding and training kennel could be made to pay. Joe's plump wife, as friendly as himself, seemed accustomed to sudden visitors. She readied the spare room and then gave Joe a report on the happenings of the day while she produced a late supper, almost without taking her eyes off the television.

When we arrived, the scenery was no more than silvery trees in the headlights and vague shapes looming in the distant dark, but I looked out of my bedroom window in the morning to see that we were in an undulating countryside of small fields, scattered trees and occasional random woodland. It was very unlike the bare and heavy hills of the west coast where my brother had his business and more akin to the softer scenery of the Lothians where I had grown up. Something told me that this was an area in which I could put down roots. I made up my mind not to let such sentiments cloud my judgment but I knew that the intangible factor of 'feeling at home', while a bad basis for decision-making, could have a profound effect on the quality of life.

Joe showed me his neat kennels and his complement of Labradors, and I met Mr and Mrs Fettle, the elderly couple who looked after the daily management. Joe seemed to have plenty of time to spare. 'But,' he said with a sideways glance, 'you can fully train a Labrador while a spaniel's still scratching itself.' He was waiting for me to point out that the Labrador, being a retriever and therefore expected to do no more than wait beside its master until there was quarry to be fetched, had little to learn beyond what a puppy did naturally, while a spaniel had to hunt without chasing, distinguish wounded game from that which was sitting tight and resist the constant temptation to chase. I denied him the satisfaction. There was even a vestige of truth in what he said. Because of their eagerness and sheer *joie de vivre*, spaniels can be hard work.

We drove to Three Oaks Farm through a straggling village which was mostly one long street of houses of various sizes and ages, a single shop, a prosperous-looking hotel and a church which was almost hidden behind trees from the passer-by.

Place-names are often illusory, being long out-dated or corruptions of words with quite different meanings, but not always. I could see the three large oaks on the skyline not far from the road, and when we turned off I found that they still stood within the new boundary.

The buildings presented a broad front to the visitor. The house itself was traditional – a single storey of grey-brown stone with a high roof of blue slates and large dormer windows lifting like frogs' eyes in silhouette. There was a substantial extension, also in stone and slate, to one side and separated from the house by a recessed porch sheltering the kitchen door. This asymmetry lent the place a pleasantly cockeyed expression, rescuing it from the severity of the typical Scottish farmhouse built to stand for ever against the worst of winters. To judge from the bolts and bars, the central front door had been little used. The house was dull and grimy, but it was dry.

Beside the extension, the gable of a barn stood and the back of the house supported several lean-to outbuildings, but the other farm buildings had been removed or demolished. A broad paddock separated the barn from the oak trees on the boundary and a small field beyond. With the example of Joe's place still fresh in my mind, I could picture the groups of kennels, each with its enclosed run.

I tried to keep my conflicting emotions out of my face. Properly developed, the place would be ideal. I could visualise several brood bitches, a dozen young dogs in training and scores of tumbling puppies. But it was a dream. Even if my half of the patrimony, supplemented by whatever I could raise on my pension, would run to it – which seemed unlikely in the extreme – the physical and mental effort would be beyond me.

'Who's the owner?' I asked.

'The same man who wants a pup off Sunbeam,' Joe said. 'Lord Craill.'

'I sold him a trained dog about two years ago,' I said.

'You seem to have sold him on spaniels altogether,' Joe said – a little sourly, I thought. 'His last Labrador's slowing up and he wants another spaniel to replace him when the old boy retires.' He looked at his watch. 'I don't want to rush you, but I have a busy afternoon ahead. And I've invited somebody to lunch.'

'Give me five minutes,' I said.

I went round once more, imagining the debris cleared away, the woodwork painted, kennels built and a garden planted and cared for. Even Moonbeam, trotting at my heels, seemed to like the place. The scents must have been propitious.

In the car, I wished that Joe had never planted the idea in my mind. It was so desirable and yet so far out of the question.

Another car was parked near Joe's front door. He slipped out of gear and coasted the last few yards to halt quietly behind it. I began to get out but he sat where he was.

'I'd better tell you something about Isobel Kitts,' he said. I closed my door again. 'I've asked her along because she might be the ideal partner for you. More to the point, you might be the ideal partner for her.

'Her husband's a very good friend of mine. He's retired

and a few years older than she is. There's no great shortage of money although they couldn't afford to pour it down the drain. Her trouble is boredom and it shows itself in taking a drink over the odds at times.'

He turned his head to look at me. He must have seen doubt in my face. 'She isn't an alcoholic,' he said quickly. 'Henry – her husband– wouldn't even want her to sign the pledge, he likes a few beers himself and they enjoy an occasional quiet pub-crawl together. She knows dogs. She qualified as a vet some years ago but she only practised for a few years before she married and it would be too late for her to start all over again now. She has all the qualifications and most of the experience that you'd want.'

'But she drinks,' I said.

Joe nodded. 'Being Henry's wife would be enough for some women, but not Isobel. When she doesn't have enough outlet for her considerable energy, she takes a few extra drams and still goes driving around the place. When she's occupied, she doesn't care whether she ever sees a drink again. Henry's scared stiff that she'll kill herself or somebody else, one of these days. He'd back her with capital just to keep her out of mischief.

'Now, come and meet her. After that, I've done all I can for you. You're on your own.'

Following him into the house, I cursed him silently for what he himself had called his 'interfering nature'. Even for the sake of capital to realise my new dream, I had no intention of becoming a boozer's therapist.

Isobel Kitts turned out to be a plumpish but still attractive woman somewhere in her middle years. She was well groomed, and was dressed – in some way which defied inexpert male analysis – perfectly for a Sunday lunch in the country. After Joe's warning I had half expected a falling-down drunk, or at least a harridan trembling from hangover, but her eyes were bright, her hand steady and her conversation coherent and cheerful. She took one sherry before lunch and carried it to the table with her.

'I've watched you compete,' she told me. 'Henry and I get to the field trials whenever we can, for old times' sake. Your dogs are always on form. And in tip-top condition, which is more than anybody could say for you.' She looked at me with an almost motherly concern. 'You don't seem to be very robust.'

'No.'

'Your war-wound,' Joe's wife said sympathetically and went on before I could correct her. 'What did you think of Three Oaks?'

I said that it could be made into the nucleus of a very fine kennels.

'That's what I thought,' Mrs Kitts said, 'given the expenditure. Of course, whether such a venture succeeded or failed might depend on whether you could go on breeding, training and handling winners.' She stopped and looked at me questioningly.

'He isn't as fragile as he looks,' Joe said. 'He could certainly do the training if you could look after the rest. It's my experience that you can teach a puppy the rudiments of retrieving without getting out of your armchair.'

'Training a spaniel to quest without chasing takes a little more application,' Mrs Kitts said severely. 'You're a lazy devil, Joe. I think that that's why you stick to Labradors.'

Joe laughed and nearly choked on his food. 'Anybody who chooses to work with spaniels,' he said, wiping his eyes, 'would make love standing up in a hammock, just to make life difficult.'

That argument lasted for the rest of the meal. Joe took our needling in good part. When Mrs Little had cleared the table, he got out pencils and paper and helped Mrs Kitts to do some forecasting. Her figures were close to what I could remember of his; perhaps erring a little less on the optimistic side, but the bottom line was still in the black.

I felt that I should ask whether they had made allowance for the business being run by an invalid and a drinker but the words would not come out. 'I don't think you've allowed enough time for bringing on some young dogs,' I said lamely.

'We're assuming that you'll do some horse-trading – if that isn't the wrong expression – with the pups from the first litters,' Joe said. He tapped one of the papers. 'That's what this item's to allow for. You should be able to trade one or two of the champion's pups for young dogs at an age for intensive training.'

'Plus some hard cash,' I said. 'That's what the item's for? Cash adjustments?'

Mrs Kitts nodded. 'If we come to an agreement, you can rely on your own judgment. But speak to me before you commit yourself,' she said. 'Read the pedigrees to me over the phone. That's all I'd need. We wouldn't want to bring in any flawed blood-lines.'

Joe grinned at me. 'Isobel reads pedigrees the way you or I can read a road sign,' he said.

They were not pressuring me, but even so I felt the need to get away before I committed myself to more than I could handle. 'Can I take those figures away and think about them?' I asked.

She pushed the notes to me. 'Do that. I'll have to do some thinking of my own and talk it over with my husband. But I think we could reach agreement. If so, you could leave most of the business side to me. And I'm not afraid of work. I'd pull my weight around the place.'

'I'm sure you would,' I said. She had a firm chin, I noticed. But I liked her, intuitively.

Joe, to my relief, said that it was time he got on the road. When I said goodbye to the two ladies they seemed confident that we would meet again. In the car, Joe refused any further discussion. 'It's up to you now,' he said. But I knew he thought that I would be a fool if I passed up the chance. I thought the same. But I also knew that I was capable of any folly of omission out of sheer inertia.

I transferred one suitcase and one spaniel to my own car,

thanked Joe sincerely and set off for my brother's home. My mind was too stimulated to let the old lassitude take over. When I pulled up at the old house on the outskirts of Helensburgh, I had almost convinced myself that I could do it. Sunbeam, heavy with pups though she was, tried to jump into my arms in celebration of my return, but for once my mind was elsewhere and she had to be content with a more casual greeting.

My brother was in his study. He was operating a firm of builders' merchants but his original training had been as an accountant. I put the figures in front of him and outlined the proposition.

He asked a hundred questions and did the figuring over again, but in the end he was satisfied. 'We don't want to get rid of you,' he said, 'but this could have been tailor-made for somebody in your position.'

'My financial position?'

'Partly. I was thinking more of somebody with your . . . attributes, searching for a career.'

'Is my state of health an attribute?'

He gave me the reproachful look which had once been reserved for a younger brother who had borrowed and lost one of his more treasured possessions. 'Handicaps are for overcoming,' he said rather pompously. 'Until you get your health back, nobody else is going to offer you a job. Self-employment's your one alternative to vegetating.'

To my surprise my sister-in-law, whom I had always suspected of resenting my presence, was the one to raise objections. 'You'd be among strangers if you fell ill again,' she said.

'They wouldn't always stay strangers,' I pointed out.

'He'd be better placed for visiting the quacks in London,' my brother said. 'And at least he'd have a partner to keep things ticking over. John, is this what you really want to do with your life?'

I surprised myself by saying that it sounded like heaven.

Or rather better, I added. The traditional view of heaven makes it sound rather a bore.

He told me to bring any draft agreement to him for vetting.

Almost before I knew it, I had committed myself, or, to be more precise, had allowed others to commit me. Everybody seemed to want a finger in the pie, so I kept my head down and let those others get on with it. It suited my mood to be carried along by their momentum. David, my brother, hammered out an agreement which he said was satisfactory and I signed without reading it.

Mrs Kitts produced her share of the necessary capital and Three Oaks was purchased, together with the small adjoining field on which I insisted. The number of dogs for which we were planning would soon have turned the smaller area of grass which came with the house into an insanitary mud-patch. Isobel Kitts also dealt with the authorities and oversaw the necessary building works. She usually consulted me by phone as a courtesy, but she proved quite capable of making decisions on her own. Joe told me that she had taken on a new lease of life. Polly, my sister-in-law, drove all the way to Fife and spent a day picking out colours.

Fortunately my illness, which some of the doctors believed to be a rare and virulent form of malaria, went into at least a partial remission. God knows I was already wearing myself out without any such additional strain on my slender store of energy. Sunbeam presented me with a large litter and between the demands of surrogate fatherhood, the problems of accommodation posed by the increasing pack, horse-trading to obtain a spectrum of ages and blood-lines and later resuming the training of my older bitches and of some new acquisitions, I had my hands full.

I spent some money – after telephonic consultation with Isobel – but we were both pleased with the results.

In particular, I came by a handsome little male springer, warranted by Isobel to be clear of any possibility of congenital defects and known by me to be of winning parentage. Samson was already half trained and shaping well. We were going to need a non-related stud dog of proven success in competition who would be in residence, so that prospective purchasers of young gundogs could see both parents at work before committing themselves to their companion and working partner for the next decade. Samson, we hoped, would grow into that duty.

In the late spring I left my sister-in-law in charge of the livestock and made what was only my fourth visit to Three Oaks. Renovation to the house was well in hand and the concrete plats had been laid which would support small clusters of individual kennels, each with its own mesh-enclosed run. But builder's debris was everywhere and I had to work hard to convince myself that order would ever emerge from the chaos.

I would have expected the stress to drive Isobel back to the bottle, but she was a model of calm assurance. She could hardly have failed to see that I was beginning to fidget. 'They're moving as fast as we've any right to expect,' she said. 'Try to have patience.'

'I'm trying,' I said. 'I'm trying very hard. But I'm getting desperately short of space. I must be in before Moonbeam's pups arrive. I need to break up the litter before one of them decides that he's the leader of the pack. That's a belief that's very difficult to eradicate once it's established.'

Isobel looked doubtful but she understood. The trainer must also be the pack leader or he is doomed to failure. 'I'll speak to the foreman,' she said. 'He's a bit of a magician. He'll probably want to saw me in half, but he may pull a rabbit out of a hat instead. You've no need to break up the litter until they're at least eight weeks old. The builders might be able to get the kitchen and one bedroom finished by then. I think enough of the kennels might be finished. If not, we'll have to improvise.'

Leaving her to argue with the men, I took a walk up the rise behind the house. As always, my mood was swinging between excitement and a conviction that we were creating a monumental white elephant. It was too late for cold feet now. Perhaps if I studied the scene from a distance I might be able to conjure up again my vision of a thriving concern.

It was a pleasant spring day. My loss of weight had made me vulnerable to cold, but there was a little warmth in the sun at last. There was a resilience in the grass which found an answering spring in my step. I only needed a dog or two for company. The pastures held sheep with their lambs and over every slight crest I saw the flicker of young rabbits going down; it would have been a chance to train for steadiness. I turned and looked back over the view. When I had first seen it, winter's dull hand had been smothering the greenness with the brown of death and bare earth. Now the scene glowed with the yellower greenery of spring. A bright splash of oilseed rape lay like sunshine on the slope of a hill.

A hedgerow slanted down the slope. As I neared it, I heard a sharp crack from the far side and a few moments later voices broke out – female voices shrill with indignation and at least one male voice trying to shout them down.

I hurried to the nearest gateway, expecting to find a crowd of a dozen or more. But there were only three human figures in the next field. The sheep were huddled together at the far end of the pasture, guarded by a rough-looking collie. A tractor was ticking over not far away.

I recognised the man with the old, single-shot .22 rifle although we had never met. Isobel, who had engaged him to plough and harrow and sow grass where the now-vanished farm sheds once stood, had also pointed him out to me as a person whom it could be unwise to cross. He was Andrew Williamson, the tenant farmer of the land thereabouts. The other two figures were female, both ladies in, I supposed, their fifties. One, the stouter, was down on her knees beside a prostrate dog and displaying a backside which looked enormous in tight trousers. She was trying to address words of comfort to the dog and recrimination to the farmer. The result was less than coherent.

The other lady, who was now silent, managed to look comparatively svelte despite an anorak, a skirt of unfashionable length and Wellingtons. She was holding a springer bitch on a leash. When I appeared, she came to meet me. The bitch, I noticed, was better groomed than either of the ladies.

'You must be Captain Cunningham,' she said hurriedly. 'Is Isobel Kitts with you? We need her services as a vet. A dog's been shot.' Her manner was concerned and yet I thought that there was a trace of malicious amusement in it.

The dog on the grass, another springer bitch, was struggling feebly and making sounds of great distress. The noise tore at something inside me but there was nothing I could do. The owner was unlikely to take the word of a stranger if I told her that it should be put out of pain at once. I turned away. 'I'll fetch Mrs Kitts,' I said.

The noise must have carried to the house – or perhaps vets develop a special sensitivity to the sound of an animal in distress. I met Isobel just beyond the gateway. She was breathing deeply after the climb but not puffing, a good omen for all the hard work ahead.

'A dog's been shot,' I told her. 'There are two ladies— '

'And I can guess who they are,' she said grimly.

She marched across the grass and knelt beside the dog which was now still. Her examination lasted for only a few seconds. 'You don't need me to tell you that she's dead,' Isobel said. 'I'm sorry.'

The kneeling woman got to her feet, bringing with her a large handbag which she held for a moment as if tempted to use it for a weapon. Her pointed face was twisted by both grief and fury. 'You'll be sorry, Andrew

Williamson,' she said shrilly. 'You did that out of nothing but wickedness. I'll make you pay for it.'

'You can try, Mrs Cory,' the farmer said. 'No doubt you'll do that. But you'll no' manage it. Yon dug was worrying my sheep.'

'You're a damned liar! We'll see what the police make of it. She was only playing,' Mrs Cory said. 'She thinks . . . thought that sheep were woolly poodles. She wanted to be friends with them. That's true, isn't it, Laura?'

'I did suggest that you kept them both on their leads,' the other said impartially. 'But, yes, that's the way I saw it.'

The farmer was unruffled, secure in the knowledge that Scottish courts allow the farmer a liberal interpretation of the word 'worrying'. 'Likely it would be, Mrs Daiches,' he said, 'seeing as you're bosom friends.' He laid a slight emphasis on the word 'bosom' and I saw the ladies flinch. Neither of them had been neglected when busts were being apportioned. He turned and looked at me. 'And what did you see? Or are you friends wi' the ladies?'

Mrs Cory focused on me for the first time through genuine tears, although whether they were tears of rage or sorrow I could only have guessed. 'You saw that she was only playing, didn't you?' she demanded.

'I've never met either of these ladies before,' I told the farmer, 'and I didn't see a damn thing. I was fifty yards the wrong side of the hedge.'

All three of them were looking at me as if I were a cowardly liar but it was Mrs Cory who took me to task. 'And I heard that you were a spaniel breeder!' she said.

'Only working spaniels,' Mrs Daiches murmured.

Alongside both embarrassment and compunction, I felt some amusement which I was careful to hide. Mrs Cory had suggested obliquely that spaniel enthusiasts should stick together to the point of perjury. Now her friend was using the word 'working' as if the divide between working and show springers was analogous to that between the human working class and the aristocracy.

'Would you like me to see to the burying of your dog for you?' I asked Mrs Cory. It seemed the least I could do.

'Certainly not!' Mrs Cory bottled up her temper and turned her mind to practicalities. 'Nobody's to touch her. I'll phone my husband to come and fetch her down to the vet – the proper vet,' she added, with a glare at poor Isobel and a vague gesture with the big handbag. 'I'll want a valuation so that I can take this . . . this animal murderer through the courts. I'll make you pay, Andrew Williamson, you see if I don't. You'll not get away with shooting a harmless spaniel. And you call yourself a farmer!'

She swung away. Mrs Daiches handed her the lead of the surviving spaniel bitch but paused. 'You'll note that I left my dogs at home,' she said to nobody in particular. 'I've never felt that they were safe when Mr Williamson was around. The man's trigger-happy. Come, Olive.' The two friends set off towards the village together.

'I do call mysel' a farmer,' Mr Williamson told me. 'And that's my way of it. I shoot any dog that chases my sheep, and you'd best mind that if you're bringing more tykes to Three Oaks. Keep them off my land.'

The land belonged to Lord Craill and I had been careful to get a letter from his lordship before agreeing to the purchase. I showed it to the farmer and then took it back and stowed it away. 'My dogs don't chase sheep,' I said. 'And I shoot any farmer who lifts a gun to one of them. That's my way of it. And don't you forget it.'

He spat on the ground, very close to my foot, and turned on his heel.

'Ho-hum!' Isobel said. 'Now you've met all your immediate neighbours.'

# THREE

I had been impatient for removal day, but in the end it came rushing at me and found me only just prepared.

My possessions were few enough that the removers scorned to bring anything larger than their smallest van. Even so, I was abashed when I saw the gaps left in the Helensburgh house by the removal of my few furnishings plus the pieces which Polly forced on me.

Walking out of the house, which had been my base and later my home ever since the death of our parents, took almost more effort than I could make. Polly and my brother were suddenly smitten with the cold feet which I thought that I was over. I promised to look after myself. And, no, I wouldn't hesitate to call for help if I needed it. And, yes, I would write.

The removers had been keen to transport every inanimate object which I owned, down to the training dummies and feeding dishes, but they had drawn the line at dogs. After considering every practical and impractical option, I had finally decided that one quick, chaotic journey would present the fewest difficulties. So I had laid flat the rear seat of the estate car, erected a garden net behind the front seats and loaded the entire menagerie into the back.

My horse-trading had increased the bulk of the two full litters without significantly reducing numbers, but dogs can curl and pack themselves into remarkably small places and none of the pups were small enough to be crushed and smothered. If there were mess, car-sickness, chewing or even a fight, they could last the rest of the journey without much more damage than could be put right by a good hosing-out. Before I passed Balloch, several of the younger litter had bypassed the net and were crawling and squeaking under my feet, but as long as they stayed out from under the pedals I let them be. Most of the remainder were asleep in one comfortable sprawl.

Isobel was waiting at Three Oaks. The builders, under her ceaseless prodding, had worked magic. More of the house was habitable than I had dared hope. Materials and scaffolding were still around but they had been stacked tidily where they could be ignored. Most of the kennels were ready; warm wooden structures with metal edgings to minimise damage by chewing. Isobel's eyes popped slightly when she saw the snoring heap of white and liver and occasional black. We set about transferring them to their newly creosoted homes, doubling them up where necessary. The task went slowly because Isobel, who had not met them before in the fur and flesh, was manipulating hips and shoulders and looking into eyes. We were only half done when the van rolled up to the front door.

'No congenital troubles so far,' she said. 'You go and see to your furniture. I'll finish up here.'

'There's no such word as "finish" in the vocabulary of a working kennel,' I said. 'By then, it'll be feeding time. It's always feeding time or cleaning-out time or walking time.'

'Or singing them to sleep time?'

'Now you're getting it,' I said.

The men were quick. The decorators had almost finished and most of my furniture could go into its destined positions. I was back with Isobel inside an hour, wheeling the trolley, formerly the property of some supermarket, which I used for the transport of feeds prepared in bulk. The spaniels abandoned the exploration of their new quarters and stood up against the chain-link mesh, willing us to hurry.

'I hope you can tell which is which,' Isobel said when the food had been distributed, 'because I'm damned if I can.'

'I'll sort them all out in the morning,' I said. 'Within a fortnight, they'll be as individual to you as your own family.' I probably sounded tired, which I was.

She looked at me much as she would, some years earlier, have studied an ailing horse. I half expected her to feel my nose. 'You don't look too hot,' she said. 'I thought you told me you were getting over your illness.'

'I was. But it comes and goes.'

She accepted that for whatever it was worth. 'Have a meal and a good night's sleep. When can I see the pedigrees of all these pups?'

'In the morning. They came on the van.'

'That's good. We'll have to sort them out into which we're selling as pups, which we're training for sale and which we're bringing on for breeding.' Samson had finished his food and was standing against the wire, hoping for attention. 'So this is our white hope,' Isobel said. I could have sworn that Samson nodded agreement. 'I've seen his pedigree, of course. Looks good.'

'He's very willing,' I said. 'He learns quickly and he never forgets. If he has a fault, he's over-eager.'

'Needs firm handling?'

'Very. Given that, and if we can get him into competition early next season, he could make a name for himself by about the end of next year.'

'But what sort of a name?' asked a voice behind us. While we were engrossed, a woman had approached us over the grass. I recognised Mrs Daiches with another of those gangling spaniels on a lead. She nodded casually to Isobel and held out her hand to me in a regal gesture. I shook it, wondering whether I was not expected to raise it to my lips. 'We've met,' she said, 'but the atmosphere was a little tense for socialising. I heard that you were moving in and I thought that I'd walk up and bid you welcome as one spaniel person to another.' She looked doubtfully at Samson.

Isobel was giving me a small, warning headshake, but I felt that the original question needed an answer. 'A name like Field Trials Champion,' I said. 'We want to use him for stud.'

Mrs Daiches looked amused. 'Do you really? But how odd! He's snub-nosed.'

So this was war. My hackles rose. I forgot about being tired. 'He may not conform to the Kennel Club's notional standards of what they think a spaniel should look like,' I said. 'But he's healthy and intelligent, two things that the show standards don't pay much heed to.'

She smiled coldly. 'It seems a pity to go out of your way to breed ugly dogs,' she said in gentle reproof. It was becoming clear that Mrs Daiches and her friend were two of a kind – argumentative women always ready for a fight – but that while Mrs Cory was a bludgeon Mrs Daiches was a rapier.

Isobel had stooped to exchange greetings with some of the pups. I guessed that she had been embroiled in such arguments in the past.

'We go out of our way to breed good working dogs,' I said. I knew that I was rising to bait but I no longer cared. 'If this is what they look like, then this is how a proper spaniel should look. If you study the old sporting prints, you'll see that my dogs resemble the original breed more than yours do.'

Her rather narrow nostrils flared suddenly. 'Don't you think that it's rather like prostitution,' she said, 'making your money by serving a bloodsport?'

There was, I knew, little point in debating with a con-firmed anti-fieldsports fanatic. How do you express a philosophy and a way of life in few enough words to hold the attention of a disbeliever? But there was a converse to her argument. At least I could strike back. 'We train spaniels to do what the breed was first developed to do. A spaniel which isn't allowed to quest and retrieve never knows fulfilment. No wonder they go odd or run wild. Or worry sheep,' I added, remembering. 'In my book, the whore is the breeder who makes money by distorting and destroying a once great breed by trying to turn a worker into a lapdog.'

My remark about sheep worrying may have been below the belt but it had its effect. 'I suppose you shoot!' she said, in a tone of voice which would have been more suitable for suggesting that I ate babies. 'But the world has moved on since the days of the grand *battues*, thank the Lord! Society won't stand for sadism as a pastime much longer.' In her agitation and the plethora of sibilants she spat slightly onto my coat. If I had felt mannerly I would have ignored it. Instead, I pulled out a handkerchief and wiped my sleeve.

She turned and stalked away. Her spaniel, which had squatted for a pee, was almost jerked off its feet.

Isobel watched her retreating back with distaste. 'I was brought up to love my neighbour,' she said. 'It isn't easy. Luckily, she's your neighbour rather than mine. Mesdames Daiches and Cory occupy the first two houses as you reach the village.'

'At least she came alone.'

'This time. The pair of them go everywhere together. We'd have had them both up, nosing around and being catty, except that Olive Cory broke a leg some months ago and I'm pleased to hear that it's giving her trouble again. Not from kicking herself, you can be sure. She's never wrong.'

'Do they breed those not unattractive mutants?' I asked.

'They do. And show them, quite successfully.' Isobel returned her full attention to me. 'Do you have food in the house?' she asked.

'Enough for tonight. My sister-in-law insisted on making me up a food-parcel.'

'That was sensible of her. If you don't feel up to cooking, you can come to us.'

'I'd rather not leave the dogs unwatched. Not with ladies like that one around.'

She nodded sombrely. 'I don't think Laura Daiches would vent her malice on us physically. Olive Cory has other things to worry about just now, but she could be capable of letting them out, just from spite. Anyway, you're right. We've got too much invested in these animals to take any chances. What we really need is a kennel-maid's chalet close to the kennels.'

The idea of another outflow of capital terrified me. 'For the moment, I have an idea for a simple system of alarms,' I said. 'Let's not do any more building until we're sure that we have a going concern.'

'We'd better be sure of that right now,' she said sharply.

Isobel Kitts turned out to be a tower of strength. I had been half prepared to find myself shackled to a sleeping, or at least a somnolent, partner. A sleeping-it-off partner would not have surprised me. But she proved to be a hard worker and not afraid to get her hands dirty. Her experience as a trainer was slight and far from recent, but she was able to relieve me on the elementary training of young dogs. Soon I was sure that I could rely on her opinion as to which dogs would be worth training for field trials. This may, in part, have been because her opinion usually coincided with my own. If we were going to be wrong, we could be wrong together.

On about my third day I left her in charge and walked down to make the acquaintance of the local doctor. He was a man nearing retirement age, white-haired, irritable as a father might be irritable, very much the traditional figure of a family doctor but a kindly man and a good and up-to-date doctor all the same. He had digested my file.

'I see that the London School of Tropical Medicine still wants to receive quarterly blood samples,' he said. 'We'd better go on with that. They may come up with something in the end.'

'And until then?' I asked.

'We can continue the palliatives. For the rest . . . I

could speak for hours, but the best advice I can give you is "Learn to live with it."' He looked at me sharply, as though I had been cursing fate.

I trailed back to the kennels and gave Isobel an evasive answer to her questions.

Several owners had left dogs with us for re-training prior to the season. While we were sharing the feeding and exercise and cleaning out, and while Isobel was also busily engaged in all the paperwork of a business which was beginning to grow, there was inadequate time for training and we would be hopelessly tied when the season of trials began.

A kennel-maid was an obvious necessity. Our first advertisement produced only one applicant, a stout girl who professed herself able and willing to undertake any of the chores. We tried her for a month and she was a disaster, lazy and far too refined to notice the accumulating plonks of dog-dirt. Rather than remove them from the grass, she preferred to take out the motor-mower – another of her duties – and mow straight over them. She then refused to clean the mower.

Her presence enabled me to take an overdue break. I was due to attend at the London School of Tropical Medicine and Isobel agreed that, having journeyed so far, I might as well head on for a break in Spain. I returned feeling strong enough to terminate the kennel-maid's contract, to the great relief of both parties.

'I have another prospect,' Isobel said a few days later. 'She worked for Joe while Mr and Mrs Fettle were visiting their daughter in Canada. Joe thinks quite highly of her.' She handed me an envelope. 'I've seen her and she impressed me favourably, but I made her write out a formal application just to be sure that she could write. She's coming up to see you tomorrow.'

'Thank God!' I said. Our training programme was beginning to falter again under the weight of seeing to the needs of so many demanding residents.

The benefit from my short holiday did not last. I felt washed out the next day and Isobel, who had adopted a motherly attitude to me, banished me to the sitting room for a midday rest. I protested at the waste of valuable time but she was adamant, so I smuggled two of the younger dogs into the house with me. As Joe had said, you can teach a pup many of the rudiments without leaving your armchair. Using an old tennis ball, I was coaxing rather than training them to wait until sent, to fetch straight back and to deliver cleanly from a sitting position when there was a tap at the door and it opened a crack.

'Mrs Kitts told me to come straight in,' a small voice said.

'Then that's what to do,' I said. 'Come along.'

A girl came in and perched uneasily on a chair. The two pups ran to her and she fussed with them. The contact seemed to put her more at ease. I noticed later that she was attractively put together. At the time, my sole impression was of extreme youth. I got the letter of application out of my pocket.

'You *are* Miss Elizabeth Cattrell?'

She nodded. 'I'm always called Beth,' she said.

'It says here that you're twenty-three.'

'That's right.'

I revised my ideas. Looking about ten years younger than your real age is not against the law, nor does it necessarily imply immaturity. I put away the letter, preferring to judge her experience by hearing her tell it.

'You worked for Joe Little?' I said.

'That's right. Just while his other staff were abroad. I moved into their cottage while they were away. Then I went back into digs in the village and helped out Mr and Mrs Spring at the boarding kennels during the busy season. But that's finished now and if I don't find something soon I'll have to go back home.' She did not sound as if home was an attractive proposition.

Her answers to my few questions were satisfactory. She seemed to know the job. She had a clean driving licence, which could be useful if Isobel went on the toot again. And, to judge by the way she fondled the dogs while we spoke, she was genuinely fond of them.

'What brought you into this area in the first place?' I asked.

'Mrs Cory advertised for help while she was laid up.'

'The broken leg,' I said. 'How did you get on with her?'

Beth hesitated, wondering whether Mrs Cory and I were friends. Her brown eyes, I decided, would have suited a spaniel. Eventually she decided on frankness, or else that nobody could possibly like the lady. 'I couldn't stand her,' she said.

I decided that Beth Cattrell would be very suitable, but there was one more test. I led her outside and showed her the motor-mower. The weather was warm and the shed was filled with the hum of flies. 'Could you mow the grass with that?' I asked.

'Yes, of course,' she said. 'I'll have to clean it first.'

I waited until we were outside before heaving a sigh of thanks. 'Start as soon as you like,' I said. 'I don't make use of the whole house. We can give you a small apartment to yourself later, but you can take over a bedroom straight away if you like. We'd prefer to have you on the premises.'

Her smile made me feel warm and strong again.

# FOUR

By the arrival of the field trials season we had our house in order, figuratively speaking. Our first selections of dogs for trialling and breeding had been confirmed and at the same time whittled down when we held an improvised simulation of a trial for ourselves, roping in every friend we could muster to act as Guns, judges and general helpers, making use of a mixture of live rabbits and previously shot, thrown pigeon as quarry – this to the vituperative indignation of Mrs Cory and the more restrained but also more biting contempt of Mrs Daiches.

The outcome, apart from some friction when we happened to meet either of our critics around the village, was that we decided to persevere with Moonbeam and to concentrate on Samson and a clever little bitch known as Scoter. Those two would be the first of the newcomers to start along the road which would lead, we hoped, through puppy stakes, novice (non-winner) stakes and open stakes towards championship status.

One of the first puppy stakes was to be held near Edinburgh and Scoter was entered.

'I think we should both go,' I said to Isobel. The three of us were doing a round of the kennels, looking for sheep ticks, ailing dogs or gaps in the mesh. 'I'll do the handling in the competition, but you should be learning the tricks of the trade. Sooner or later we're going to find that we want two dogs competing at different events on the same day.'

'Agreed,' Isobel said. Beth nodded. She had already

proved more than capable of looking after the kennels on her own.

We finished our tour at Scoter's kennel. 'You'll have to be on the ball on Saturday, my darling,' Isobel said.

'I will,' I said. 'I will.'

'I was talking to the dog,' she pointed out with mock indignation. We were all in a rather silly mood that lovely day. Business had been picking up as the shooting season dawned. Some of our surplus had been taken off our hands at fancy prices and the future seemed as rosy as the first tints of autumn which were staining the upper reaches of the oaks. And the builders had at last made a total departure, leaving the whole place pristine and uncluttered.

'Foiled again,' I said. 'I think I'll take Scoter out with the gun for an hour and remind her that she doesn't know it all. Of course,' I added, 'shooting is a cult.'

They had come to recognise the trivial humour which came over me when my health was on the up-swing and the dogs were in good fettle. 'What sort of a cult?' they asked in unison.

'Diffi-cult,' I said and they groaned, again in unison.

'If you make puns like that in front of Scoter,' Isobel said, 'she'll lose respect for you and run wild in the trial. I see a door,' she added.

'What kind of a door?' Beth and I asked.

'A Labra-door.' And when we looked, Joe Little was walking across the grass with one of his Labs at heel.

'Really, Mrs Kitts!' Beth said. 'You're as bad as he is.' Beth never quite came to terms with the fact that her two employers sometimes talked like schoolchildren.

Joe, who had not visited us for some months, made some approving comments on our set-up before coming to the point. 'You're competing on Saturday?' he asked me.

'God and the weather permitting,' I said.

'Friday, they're running retrievers,' Joe said. 'I'm judging. I've just had a phone-call. The other judge has gone down with a thrombosis and they can't find a replacement for the

Friday – the trial clashes with two other events. Saturday's no problem. You're a List B judge, aren't you?'

'Correct,' I said. It had often been impossible to run a dog during my army service and I had filled the void by acting as a judge in minor events.

'Well, would you stand in on Friday?'

I looked at Isobel. 'If I did, I'd prefer to stay over rather than do the extra driving twice. Would you rather drive yourself through on Saturday morning? Or stay away?'

'I'll come with you,' she said. 'I'd like to watch you officiating in your wig and robes.'

I saw Joe preparing to point out that she was thinking of a different sort of judge before he realised that it was her idea of a joke. He recommended a particular hotel and promised to book two rooms. 'It won't do you any harm to be reminded how it looks from the judge's standpoint,' he said.

After he left, I remembered to ask Beth whether she would be nervous if left alone overnight.

'Not in the least,' she said. She had seated herself cross-legged on the grass, picking small weeds out of the turf. Now she stood up in one lithe movement. 'I'll put Scoter's dish and two bags of mixed meal in the car before you leave. And now I must get going. I need a tree.'

'What sort of a tree?' I asked in all innocence.

'A lavva-tree.' And she said it absolutely straight-faced.

We gaped after her. 'Was that an accident or is that girl developing a sense of humour?' I asked.

'She's developing something,' Isobel said. 'I wouldn't care to put a name to it.' She spluttered with sudden laughter.


My stint as a judge seemed to pass off satisfactorily. At least I drew no more than the usual number of dirty looks from handlers excluded from the list of awards, and no outright accusations of bias. I had enjoyed my day with its moment of power.

39

But that evening, in an old-fashioned hotel remarkable for its restrained comfort and comparatively modest prices, I began to feel the weakness, lightheadedness and shivers of my old trouble. I said nothing to Isobel and made an excuse to take an early night, leaving her to chat the evening away with Joe. In the morning I felt, if anything, worse.

Isobel, when I met her at breakfast, noticed immediately. 'You've lost ground,' she said. 'Did yesterday over-tire you?'

'I don't think tiredness has much effect. It just comes and goes. If there's any pattern, I've never been able to see it.' I helped myself to some cereal which I did not want while I made up my mind. 'You'll have to handle Scoter in the trial,' I said at last.

For the first time, her quiet confidence faltered. 'I couldn't,' she said.

'You must. Dogs have an instinct for knowing when you're not on top of the job. And Scoter's already inclined to wonder if she doesn't know best. You've done as much with her in training as I have. And you've come on a mile in the last few months.'

'That isn't the same as handling in competition.'

'It's exactly the same,' I told her, not altogether truthfully. 'Just stay cool and think of the best way to make her do whatever the judges want. At least the ground and the crop pattern are similar to home. That always helps to settle a dog down quickly.'

'But you're the one who's entered.'

'It's the dog who's entered. They'll let us change handlers. If you won't do it, we'll have to withdraw. Who'll buy a dog off us if I handle her and make a balls of it?'

'We don't want to withdraw,' she said quickly. 'This isn't one of your tricks?' She looked and saw that I had pushed away my cereal untouched and was nibbling at the edge of a piece of toast. 'No, I can see that it isn't.'

'Come outside as soon as you've finished breakfast,' I said. 'We'd better let Scoter blow off steam and then you

40

can have a run through the training exercises together.'

All the way out to the ground she protested. She would never manage. She wouldn't understand the judges. She wasn't dressed for it. She didn't know the rules. When I reassured her on one point she switched to another. But once she was among other competitors, some openly nervous and others trying unsuccessfully to hide their nerves, a calm came over her and her chin went up. I took my place among the spectators. I would have preferred to doze in the car, but I felt that two of my pupils were on trial. I had two sweaters under my coat and a stick to sit on. I would survive.

Fortunately for her nerves, Isobel drew a low number and went out early. The spectators were well back from the line, but through my binoculars it seemed to me that Scoter's assurance was making up for any uncertainty on Isobel's part. But I could sense trouble ahead. Scoter was always inclined to take charge, given the chance.

Scoter's first bird was easy, a hen pheasant which she kicked up out of some bracken. The nearer Gun stopped it dead in the air and it was an easy retrieve from the open.

The line moved on through a narrow strip of kale. The stewards let us move forward. A rise in the ground gave us a better view. The other dog under the judges put out a hare which raced across the front and vanished over a ditch and through a hedge. Scoter pushed up a cock pheasant. The Gun muffed it. The cock spiralled down, a strong runner, and went ahead over an embankment and into some rushes. The judge said something and Isobel sent Scoter after it. The spaniel hurried forward but before she could pick up the scent of the pheasant she met the line of the hare and turned onto it. She knew that she had been sent for a pheasant, but dogs' memories are short and Scoter had a special penchant for hares.

Isobel whistled once. Scoter, who was getting out of hand, ignored the signal. Isobel stood there, shading her eyes and gazing towards where the pheasant had vanished.

If I had felt stronger, I would have danced with impatience. In Isobel's place I would have whistled until I burst my cheeks – knowing only too well that I would have drawn the judges' attention to the fact that the dog was out of control. Knowing, too, that the more I whistled and was ignored the worse Scoter would get.

Scoter arrived at the ditch and hedge and checked. Isobel whistled. Scoter turned, recognised a signal and started back. She picked up the cock's scent and plunged down the bank.

'That was clever,' a voice said in my ear.

'Which?' I asked without lowering my binoculars.

'Your partner. The wee bitch was headstrong but the judge was watching the bird. Mrs Kitts waited until she was ready to turn.'

Scoter came back over the crest of the embankment with the cock struggling in her jaws. As Isobel took it and I relaxed, breathing as deeply as though I had done both the handling and the retrieve, I looked round and recognised the speaker. He was stocky and sparsely red-haired and he kept the village shop with his wife. West, I remembered. Ian West. He had a young spaniel on a lead.

'It's the first trial for both of them,' I said.

He raised his eyebrows. 'Then you've a winning combination in prospect,' he said.

'Do you compete?' I asked.

'I don't even shoot nowadays, except rats with an airgun if they come near the shop. Andy here isn't even of a working strain, are you, old thing?' He stooped to pat the dog's head and it leaned affectionately against his leg. They had the mutually absorbing relationship which sometimes develops between a one-dog man and a one-man dog. 'But I like fine to watch good dogs working when I get the chance. My sister lives just up the road from here, so when there's a trial on I leave my wife to mind the shop and get a lift through for the weekend. I don't drive. Never learned and never felt the need.'

'We can give you a lift back if you like,' I said.

'No need. I'm going back with Mr Little. Came through yesterday with Laurie Duffus.' He saw that the name meant nothing to me. 'Lives next door to Mrs Daiches,' he said. 'He owns the market garden.'

'I don't think I've met him.'

'You've met him, all right,' Ian West said. 'You've certainly met him. You put him out, yesterday, for chasing. Hopping mad he was, last night. Wanted me to promise that I'd never sell you any more of his vegetables.'

I remembered the dog. The handler was vaguer in my mind although I recollected a faint sensation of *déjà vu*. 'I dare say he'll get over it in a year or two,' I said.

Isobel and Scoter were in the run-off to decide third and fourth places. They were squeezed out by more experienced handlers but Isobel was over the moon to be awarded a Certificate of Merit. As I told her several times in the car, for a dog and handler both competing for the first time it was a better result than I had dared to hope for.

'Was I really good enough?' she asked.

'Scoter's a headstrong little devil and she takes advantage whenever she can,' I said. 'You stayed calm and thought it out while I'd have gone off at half-cock. A little more practice and a determination that the game was going to be played according to Isobel Kitts and you'd have won hands down.'

Isobel was driving. 'I managed. I did all right,' she said suddenly, convinced for the first time. 'Let's stop and have dinner.'

After my day in the fresh air, at least some of my appetite was returning. 'All right,' I said. 'The Forth Bridge Motel's just ahead.'

She made the tricky turn-off. 'The drinks are on me,' she said.

While she sank two large vodkas with tonic in the bar, I carried my beer to a telephone and called Beth to tell her that we would be late and not to make a meal for me. 'We did all right,' I told her.

'I know. Mr West phoned his wife and she called me. Why was Mrs Kitts doing the handling?'

'I was a bit pooped after yesterday,' I said.

'Oh.' There was a short silence while Beth thought about it. 'You try to do too much. If Mrs Kitts is good – and Mr West said that she was very good – can't you leave the travelling around to her, at least until you're really better?'

'I might do just that,' I said. 'Anyway, don't wait up for me.'

Isobel bought a bottle of wine to go with the meal, drank most of it herself and followed it up with a brandy.

When we left, she was still in command of herself, still a lady, walking almost straight and speaking with hardly a slur, but mellow. I took over the driving. In the car, she sat silent. I thought that she might be asleep.

As we neared the village, she stirred. 'Let's go up and see that all's well at the kennels,' she said.

'No need,' I said. 'I phoned Beth.'

'But I'd like to.'

It would have been difficult to refuse her anything that night. 'All right. One of us can run you home.'

'I could walk it,' she said. 'But Henry's in London on business.'

'Use the spare bedroom,' I suggested. Isobel had drunk too much to walk home, let alone spend the night in an empty house.

All was indeed well with the dogs. We put Scoter away for the night with her rosette pinned up over the kennel. I felt ready to curl up on the straw beside her. But we walked back to the house. Beth seemed to have gone to bed.

Isobel was slightly unsteady and I felt as weak as water. We helped each other up the stairs. I nodded towards Beth's door and put a finger to my lips. Isobel nodded.

44

She followed me into my room and closed the door.

'You need looking after,' she said.

I was ready to drop. When she began to help me off with my clothes I was only grateful. I rolled naked between the sheets.

She undressed quickly and got in beside me.

# FIVE

Somebody once described their life as being like a good wine, improving with age. In my life, the only resemblance was to a cloudy wine, opaque when disturbed but clearing as it settled.

Life seemed to be clarifying at last. I got to know our neighbours and established friendships with some and scratchy relationships with others.

My health, still as changeable as the weather, remained the only variable. Sometimes I was sure that I had shaken off my malady, at other times I was certain that only death would end it. Once I got so low that I was taken into hospital and forcibly nursed back into some semblance of health.

Isobel worked with the dogs until she could handle them better than I could. We had our successes and our failures. If the world did not beat a path to our door, at least it produced its cheque-book from time to time. As our name became known, the prices our dogs fetched began an upward curve. Our expenditure on dogfood, which had at first seemed a crushing enemy, became no more than a paper tiger. At the end of the first year we declared a small dividend over and above our tiny salaries and we celebrated with a party on the grass which was attended by eighteen people and thirty-two dogs.

From that point onward, the year began to repeat itself. No longer was each day a fresh adventure with new challenges. It seemed that the seasons would roll round for ever, becoming as familiar as old shoes, too comfortable for change. A life of peaceful endeavour would suit me better than a prolonged stagger from crisis to crisis, but I wondered how long Isobel would last before repetition became monotony and drinking once again became an escape rather than a celebration. For the moment, she was buoyed up by her occasional successes in competition.

Our partnership was halfway through its second year when the tranquillity of our existence was blown to the winds. Isobel and Beth were away and I was training three dogs on The Moss, quite unaware of the violence which had scrambled my neighbours' lives, when the stranger made his appearance.

I pushed the dummy down onto the spigot of the dummy launcher, inserted the blank cartridge and gripped the launcher firmly. When I released the plunger the cartridge fired, the launcher kicked against my hand, the dummy sailed out over The Moss and three spaniels sat down hard.

The man who had just emerged from behind the remains of a tumbledown cottage nearly did the same. I dropped the ear-protectors, which had muffled his approaching footsteps, to hang round my neck. Army service had done enough damage to my hearing; I tried to protect what was left of it.

'That made me jump!' the man said, laughing at himself rather than showing any real anger. He was a man of about my age and height but more heavily built, even allowing for the weight which I had lost and which Dr Harper's regime had failed to put back onto me. His face was square and neither friendly nor unfriendly although I thought that I detected the sort of self-confidence which stops just short of arrogance. The better NCOs had had just the same air of calm self-sufficiency. His dark suit and overcoat were not what I would have chosen for a country walk on a chill December morning, but his boots were sensible.

'I'm sorry,' I said. 'It does make a hell of a bang. The locals are used to it.'

'I expect so.' His faint accent did not belong locally to Fife but came from somewhere further north. 'For a moment, I thought I'd been shot. Perhaps my mind was running on shooting.' He paused but when his words provoked no reaction he went on. 'They call this area Yappy Valley, don't they?'

The nickname always annoyed me. Yapping would never be tolerated in a working gundog. 'Excuse me a moment,' I said. 'I'd better recover that dummy before it's lost for ever.'

'Yes, of course.'

Distracted by his arrival, I had lost sight of the dummy. I sent Brutus for it. Scoter usually preferred to be directed by hand signals while Suzie would have made for the general area and then used her excellent nose. Brutus was by far the best at marking a fall. He went straight out, came back with a rush and delivered the red dummy, sitting.

If the newcomer was impressed, he gave no sign of it except for a raised eyebrow. 'You'd be Captain John Cunningham, from Three Oaks Kennels?'

'*Mr* Cunningham,' I said. The retention of my army rank, after my retirement on grounds of ill-health, would not only have suggested a more successful career, afloat or in the air, but would have reminded me of a phase of my life which I had mostly enjoyed but which I thought better forgotten.

'My name's Flodden.' He looked at me curiously. 'You know, if I'd been an infantry captain wounded in the Falklands and invalided out, I think I'd be proud enough of it to go on calling myself Captain.'

I sighed. 'That's a fiction perpetuated by my neighbours,' I said. I paused but he waited. I could only be grateful that somebody was willing to let me set the record straight for once. 'I can't think why. And it doesn't seem to matter how often I tell them. I was in the Falklands and I came through unscratched. Then I was sent to Nicaragua as an observer and I picked up some tropical bug which still baffles the quacks.'

He nodded once, slowly, as though my explanation made sense to him. 'I tried the house but there was nobody around. I met a man on a tractor near your gates and he said that he'd seen you coming this way.'

He seemed to be in no hurry to state his business. I decided that he was probably a prospective customer in search of a puppy. If I had known then what I learned later I might have made a better guess as to his mission, but at that moment the world was still peaceful and uncomplicated. His clothes did not suggest a field trials enthusiast nor, despite his opening words, a shooting man and I doubted whether he could readily spare the considerable cost of a fully trained dog although sometimes appearances could be deceptive. (When an unlikely purchaser pulls a roll of notes out of his pocket, I know that a successful poacher is after a dog which can be worked in silence.)

I decided that direct questions might put him off. I would let him work round to what he wanted at his own pace. In the meantime, if he wanted to hang around he could damn well make himself useful.

'How would you like to give me a hand?' I asked.

'I'm game – if it's within my skill, which is unlikely.'

'A ten-year-old boy could do this for me. In fact, one sometimes does when he's around. Suzie – the little black and white bitch – was sent to me because she was unsteady to fur.'

He looked puzzled. Perhaps he wasn't a prospective client after all. Or maybe he wanted a guard dog trained or a house pet cured of chewing the furniture, in which case he would be doomed to disappointment. 'She was what?'

'She chased rabbits,' I explained. 'I've been retraining her on the lawn, using rabbit-skin dummies and miles of elastic. Now I want to know if I've done the trick, but we had the myxomatosis around here in the autumn and the rabbit population's at an all-time low just now. The few survivors are underground and showing no signs of wanting to come out and lend a hand. What I want is to send her out for a dummy and to have you fire another one along the ground in front of her as she comes back. Could you manage that?'

'I should think so.'

'Try not to hit her with it. I once hit a dog with a dummy, accidentally. He limped for a week and I had to spend a month giving him his confidence back.'

I showed him the mechanism. He tried to look through the hole in the spigot and seemed disappointed to discover that it did not go straight to the end. I took it back and fired a dummy as far as it would go, about eighty yards across the rough ground. The Moss, being in part rocky and partly too boggy to plough, was ideal for dog training, a mixture of grassy areas with every variety of self-sown bushes and reeds.

I dug another dummy, this one covered with rabbit-skin, out of my shoulder-bag.

'Let me see if I can load it,' he said. 'Give me the blank cartridge.'

'Put the dummy on first,' I told him. 'Otherwise the air pressure makes it difficult to push down.' I watched carefully while he readied the device. He seemed to have the idea. 'You'd better take your gloves off,' I said. 'Woollen gloves are slippery and the launcher has quite a recoil. You can stave a thumb easily if you don't take a good grip.' I showed him how to hold it back-handed so that it would kick against the butt of his fist. 'Now, you go and stand near that old tree-stump. Try to bounce the dummy across in front of her as she comes back.'

When he was in place, I sent Suzie out. She bustled across the grass, her short tail going like a fly-whisk, cast about for a few seconds and then pounced on the dummy. When she was halfway back, the other shot sounded and the rabbit-skin dummy bounced realistically across her front. She checked in her stride but came on again and delivered to my hand. I could have sworn that Scoter and Brutus both relaxed approvingly. Scoter set herself to go for the rabbit-skin dummy so I sent Brutus instead. I was still determined to impress on Scoter that her function in life was to obey orders.

Flodden rejoined me and handed me back the launcher. 'You were right,' he said. 'It does have a kick. Was that what you wanted?'

'Perfect,' I said. 'I think we'll knock off now while we're winning. Always finish on a triumph – that's a good motto in dog training.'

His smile was faint and gone almost before I noticed it. 'It's a good motto in life. I'll adopt it for my coat of arms, when they give me one. I'll walk back with you, if I may,' he said.

He was definitely not a customer but as long as he was prepared to be useful he was welcome to hang around.

Our walk back to the kennels followed a farm track between hedges. The damp and unproductive ground of The Moss gave way to fields, a patchwork of grass, winter barley, rape and the brown corduroy furrows of plough. A small field of kale was taking punishment from a flock of hungry pigeon. In the clear air, the nearer hills looked close and sharp but a swell of the ground hid the village. I let the dogs go out in front but kept an eye on them, ready to call them to order if they began to hunt or to eat anything altogether too revolting.

'There seem to be rather a lot of dog breeders around here,' my companion said suddenly.

I shrugged although he was watching the dogs at the time. 'Only three that you could consider to be professionals. You get amateurs everywhere. Anyone who owns a bitch or two can be a breeder for the money. That's what I was doing before I moved here. But you need a bloodline with a list of successes behind it to make a business. Being near each other's very convenient,' I finished. 'We can help each other out in times of stress.'

'No jealousies?'

'Very little between the pros. We're not in competition. Joe Little goes in for Labradors. Mr and Mrs Spring run a boarding kennel and breed Jack Russells. Several families in the village have a bitch or two which they breed from in an amateur or semi-amateur sort of way.'

'There are spaniels at the Daiches kennels and the house opposite,' he pointed out.

'Mrs Daiches and Mrs Cory breed springers for the show bench,' I explained. 'Several amateurs breed spaniels for show around here. I don't count them as competition. I barely count them as dogs. They don't go in for field trialling.'

'Some competition for buyers there, surely?'

Scoter was hunting for rabbits along a bank covered with dead bracken. I called her off. 'If somebody wants a spaniel for a pet,' I said, 'they can get a pup from Mrs Daiches or Mrs Cory and the best of luck to them. I wouldn't sell them one. Mine are workers.' And I waited to see whether that would put him off.

'I see,' he said, after a pause. 'And what brought you here?'

He was very inquisitive, but I have always preferred my life to be an open book. Secrecy only encourages speculation. 'When I left the army,' I said, 'my only assets were a little cash, a small pension and a pair of very well pedigreed young spaniel bitches which my brother had been keeping for me.'

'And a knack for training dogs?'

'I liked to think so.' My military colleagues had sometimes accused me of training the men as if they were gundogs, but I rarely fell into the mistake of treating the dogs as people. 'I lived with my brother for a while and entered a few field trials. I fluked a few wins and was offered dogs to train. I spent some money on stud fees and knew that the pups would sell well if I trained them on. I started wondering about a place of my own. I met Joe Little when he was judging a spaniel trial – though just who ever thought that a Labrador man could judge spaniels I don't know. I was asked to judge a retriever trial last year, but that's different.'

'Why is it different?' my visitor asked. He sounded amused.

Either he knew very little about dogs or he was sounding me out. 'Retrieving is retrieving, whichever breed does it. But retrievers don't quest for game. Not in competitions, anyway. They just hang around waiting for beaters and spaniels to do the hard work. Joe mentioned that the Three Oaks farmhouse was on the market. It was ideal. There was enough land, plenty of rough ground round about and a supply of local ladies to help out at busy times. We get by.'

We had joined the road, which had once been an important route but now only carried local traffic. My drive came off at a bend above the village. He followed me up past the house and watched as I sat the dogs and sent them into their kennels one by one. There was some whining and whickering from the other kennels.

The kennels and their associated runs were shaded in summer and sheltered in winter by two of the big oak trees. The third, to my great regret, had blown down in a big gale during the previous winter. The trunk had been sold for timber but the branches were still present in the form of a neat pile of seasoning logs. Although we had planted a replacement oak it would be generations before the new one was a match for the others.

The kennels were arranged in groups of four or six, to prevent the spread if a disease should get a foothold, and a separate isolation kennel stood nearer to the house. Each kennel had its concrete run with an escape-proof fence. Concrete paths now linked the kennels with each other and with the house. And Beth had expended some of her spare time in planting flowering shrubs. The prospect was becoming one which, even in mid-winter, brought me a little quiet pride whenever I had time to notice it.

My visitor looked around him and made a small noise to himself, but I could not have told whether he was impressed or contemptuous. I could have hurried him into stating his business but, truth to tell, I was tired. My illness seldom bothered me, but talking about it seemed to have reminded it of my existence and I was feeling whacked. The stranger had been helpful and might be helpful again.

'I must get on,' I said. 'I have two litters of puppies to feed.'

'I'll give you a hand,' he said quickly. 'You look washed out. You surely don't run a place this size on your own?'

'Lord no!' I said, as we walked to the house. 'I have a partner – Mrs Kitts – and a kennel-maid. But Mrs Kitts is away running our best dog in a qualifying trial at the moment – I want to make him up to Field Trials Champion. I have more patience than she has for training but she has the stamina and the calm determination for serious competition.'

'And the kennel-maid's let you down?'

'Beth goes along as chauffeur and general dogsbody,' I said. I felt no call to explain that Isobel Kitts, who could remain as steady as a rock while controlling a headstrong dog under the judges' eyes, was still inclined to unwind after the competition, celebrating a success or drowning a failure in the company of any other competitors brave enough to drink with her. Beth, who I sometimes suspected of being slightly retarded but who was an excellent driver, accompanied her to ensure that the dog and, if possible, Isobel arrived home safely.

In the feed room, which adjoined the kitchen, I showed my visitor what to do and he mixed puppy-meal while I made coffee for both of us and a sandwich for myself.

Food usually restored my energy but without putting any flesh back on my bones.

Feeling slightly better, I led the way back to the kennels, carrying a stack of plastic bowls while my unexplained helper lugged the bucket of warm meal. Both litters were still with their dams although the bitches no longer had milk. I still carried the dummy launcher and I fired a blank before I fed them. The greedy pups guzzled and squabbled over the dishes. I was watching the agitated little creatures milling around in competition for the most advantageous feeding position, but my visitor was casting his eye around.

'What did you fire the shot for?' he asked.

'If they associate the sound of a shot with something pleasant, like food, they're much less likely to be gun-shy or nervous later.'

He nodded to himself. He seemed ready to absorb an incredible amount of ill-assorted information. 'Are these all your own dogs, then?' he asked.

'About half,' I said. 'We breed, we sell pups, we train and sell and we keep what we hope will turn out to be the very best for future competition and breeding. Sometimes we get it right. Most of the rest have been brought to me for training.'

'You don't take boarders, then?'

'Not usually, as such, unless it's to take the overflow from Mr and Mrs Spring. They tend to be fullest in the summer when we're at our emptiest. Sometimes we oblige somebody special. Lord Craill, for one.'

'Because he's a lord?'

'Because he's a bloody good customer. He's bought two dogs off me already. He never has less than four around the place, so I can probably count on selling him a dog every three years or so. When the season's over, he shoots rabbits over them until he's made them as wild as tigers. Then he dumps them on me, plus several cats, and buggers off abroad for the summer and he expects me to convince his blasted dogs that they're not greyhounds after all. I'm supposed to have them steady again by the time the grouse season opens. Why he can't keep two for the rabbits and two for game I don't bloody well know,' I finished indignantly.

He was grinning at me. 'But it's money in the bank.'

'At least he pays his bills,' I agreed. I was still watching, to be sure that no pup was being bullied out of its share and because I enjoyed the sight of a good litter of pups at feed. There is no happier creature on earth than a feeding puppy and some of their happiness always rubbed off on me.

'It all sounds like a lot of work. What time did your partner leave this morning?'

'They went last night,' I said. 'Friday. Samson doesn't always travel well by car.' It struck me belatedly that his questions had strayed over the bounds of mere curiosity. 'Just who are you and what are you after?' I asked bluntly.

'I told you my name.'

My skin began to prickle. On active service, that had meant that something was wrong. Once, it had saved me from a sniper. 'You've told me just about damn-all. Now you can tell me what you really want, Mr Flodden.'

He sighed, quite unembarrassed. 'Sergeant Flodden,' he said, 'CID. Let's go and take a seat on that bench. You're looking peaky again. Or would you rather go indoors?'

My coat was warm. I preferred the cool, fresh air when I was feeling off-colour. And I felt a sudden revulsion against taking this Judas into my home again. 'The bench will do,' I said.

# SIX

The bench was under one of the oaks – a shady spot in summer although cold in December. But at least one could rest the legs. We settled ourselves and I pulled my coat tighter around me.

'Are you supposed to ferret out a lot of gossip without telling people who you are?' I asked him.

He half-smiled with what I had at first taken to be an honest and open face. Any likeableness in his features was now buried under that maddening air of self-sufficiency. 'I'm supposed to gather information as best I can. As far as I am aware, you said nothing that should be regretted by yourself – or anybody else,' he said. He spoke with the soothing tone which one uses to children and the very old. 'If you had, it couldn't be used in evidence. That's the only difference it makes. If you think back, you'll see that I didn't tell you any lies. I just put off telling the whole truth for half an hour. If it offended you, well, that's a pity. But people often talk less freely once they know they're talking to the police. Not necessarily because they have anything to hide. They just feel inhibited.

'You, for instance. You gave me an interesting picture of how the dog business works. It may prove to be irrelevant, you understand, but interesting. And you threw a little light on some of your neighbours. Would you have done that if I'd introduced myself as CID?'

'I think I would,' I said. I leaned back against the tree-trunk. 'I was brought up to believe that the policeman was my friend. Until just now, I never had reason to doubt it. So what's it all about? What am I supposed to have done?'

'You took your time getting around to that question. Are you sure you don't know?'

I cast around in my mind but there was nothing on my conscience nor had I witnessed any crime or suffered any wrongdoing. 'I've not the faintest idea,' I said.

'Very odd.' He seemed to be weighing my words for implications of which, if they existed at all, I was quite unaware. 'I'll ask you again. What time did Mrs Kitts and your kennel-maid leave here yesterday?'

'Fiveish. After the chores were finished.'

'Leaving you alone in the house?'

'Yes.'

He produced a notebook and began to write. 'What did you do after that?' he asked.

The matter, whatever it might be, was beginning to look serious and close to home. The oaks grew out of a slight rise and the bench was sited to give a view over the village which, I noticed, seemed busier than usual. A large caravan was parked on unploughed stubble beside the first house. 'I think you should tell me what this is about,' I said.

'Bear with me a little longer. Your next few answers may be crucial and they'll carry more conviction if you don't try to tell me what you think I want to be told. After that, I'll explain.'

After a moment's thought I decided that I, like Brutus, was armed so strong in honesty that threats could pass me by. (A Channel Four production of *Julius Caesar* had been shown a few nights earlier and some of the lines were still running through my head. My mind, as so often when I had tired myself out, flitted around like a butterfly. I wondered what the Sergeant's face would do if I invited him to digest the venom of his spleen, but decided not to bother.)

'Very well,' I said. 'Mrs Kitts and I had been giving Samson a final polish, reminding him of who's the leader of the pack. We fed the other dogs together, filled the water dishes and gave the pens a last clean. Then they went off in my car. Mrs Kitts had brought her overnight case here with her. Beth left me a meal in the oven. After I'd eaten as much of it as I could manage, I took some of what I call my junior class into the barn for some elementary training work by artificial light. That was my advanced class you met this afternoon.'

'What were you teaching your primary pupils?'

'Simple retrieving. Sitting to the sound of a shot. That sort of thing.'

'Using the dummy launcher?'

'Using a blank cartridge pistol,' I said. 'The blanks are cheaper and about as loud indoors as the dummy launcher is in the open.'

'And after that?'

'I was tired. I went to bed. Alone. Now, what the hell is all this about?'

He looked at me for a few seconds, mentally calculating whether the optimum moment had arrived for revelations. Evidently it had. But even his revelations took the form of a question. 'Nobody told you that there was a murder in the village?'

'I haven't seen anybody,' I said.

'And no phone calls?'

'The only calls that came in were long-distance – an enquiry about the price of a pup and a plea from a former client wanting advice about a false pregnancy. His bitch, not his wife. Who was murdered?'

He shot me another probing look. Perhaps because I was preoccupied as usual with my own troubles, I had been rather late in asking a question which would have been at the forefront of a less self-centred man's mind.

'Early this morning,' he said at last, 'Mrs Daiches was found lying dead in her own back garden. We don't have a pathological report yet, but first indications are that she died yesterday afternoon or early evening.'

'Poor old thing,' I said quietly. That explained the position of the caravan. Mrs Daiches and her husband occupied the first house on the left as you entered the village, with Mr and Mrs Cory opposite. I wanted to ask how she had been killed but the Sergeant, while maintaining an appearance of frankness, was in fact measuring out his own disclosures with a teaspoon; and I was unsure whether I could absorb any gory details without disgracing myself. 'You can't have been on the job for very long. What brings you beating a path to my door?'

'I'm only one of half a dozen,' he said. 'If we don't make an arrest soon, the number will go up dramatically. For the moment, until the forensic lads have done their stuff and a search of the garden and surroundings is finished, we're visiting those who are known to have quarrelled with the lady. From your tone of voice, you didn't like her very much?'

It had always been too late to deny it. 'You'll be interviewing her antagonists until the cows come home,' I said. I sighed. 'This doesn't seem to be the occasion for being mealy-mouthed about the dead.'

'It isn't. This is very much the occasion for being absolutely frank instead of leaving us to draw inferences.' He was looking me squarely in the eye and I thought that he might be trying to give me a well-intentioned warning. 'And you seem to have made your views too well known for any attempt at evasion.'

'I wasn't alone in my opinion of her. She was an old bitch with bees in her bonnet. Not the screaming, fishwife sort of bitch like her friend Mrs Cory, unless you pushed her too hard. More of a supercilious bitch with an edge to her tongue.' It occurred to me that I might have said too much. 'I take it that Mrs Cory is still walking around?'

'She is,' he said. 'Why?'

'If I had been going to shoot either of them, it would have been Mrs Cory.'

'Why do you say "shoot"?'

I had to think before I remembered. 'You said earlier that your mind was running on shooting.'

'So I did.' There was a pause while he wrote that down. 'You had a stand-up row with Mrs Daiches in the hotel.'

I wondered which of my neighbours had been spiteful and decided that Mrs Cory would have been the tale-bearer.

'More than one,' I said. 'So did almost everybody else in the place, and especially every other dog-owner for miles around. I'd like to be able to say that we debated rather than had rows, but truth to tell our debates always degenerated into shouting-matches. I think she enjoyed them.'

'And you didn't?'

'I hate arguing with bigots. She had strong views about everything from politics to the best way to boil a cabbage, but strongest of all about dogs. As far as she was concerned, she was right and everybody else was wrong and she never hesitated to tell the world about it.'

The information did not seem to surprise him. It seemed that Mrs Cory, the lady with the hyperactive and venomous tongue, had at least been impartial in her tittle-tattle. 'What was the subject of your last quarrel?' he asked.

He would certainly have been told the bone of my contention with Mrs Daiches. But I doubted whether he had fully understood it and I enjoy grinding axes as much as the next man. 'We both breed springer spaniels,' I said. 'But you'd hardly have known them for the same breed. As I told you, mine are workers, bred from good working dogs with the blood of Field Trials Champions among them. They're bred for strength and vigour and intelligence. They go to shooting men or into field trials.

'Mrs Daiches, like her friend Mrs Cory, thought that shooting was barbarous and that dogs should be man's best friend and nothing more. To them, rabbits were cuddly bunnies and pheasants our feathered friends.' I knew that my tongue was running away with me, making many of the points which I had made to the late Mrs Daiches, but I was quite unable to stop myself ranting. 'Her spaniels were bred as pets and for the show-bench, without a worker in the pedigree. They were bred to conform with certain arbitrary standards of appearance set by the Kennel Club. Bred, in fact, to be beautiful, with only token attention paid to good health and none at all to brains. As a result of that sort of breeding, springers, like some other breeds, are becoming almost two separate breeds which you can tell apart at a glance from half a mile off. The large ones which fall over when they try to scratch themselves are the show-bench dogs.'

'Yes. I can quite see that you wouldn't enjoy arguing with bigots,' he said. He was laughing at me.

I shrugged off the implication. 'As anybody will tell you, Sergeant, and probably already did, I feel about show-breeding as the feminists feel about beauty contests. Rather more strongly, in fact, because dumb, haemophiliac blondes aren't being bred specially with Miss World titles in view, but a good breed is being endangered for the sake of a few trophies and a lot of cash.

'In other words, Mrs Daiches thought that what I was doing was wrong and I knew that what she was doing was damnable. These are subjects which dog people can get hot under the collar about, but I wouldn't have killed her over it and I don't think that she would have killed me.'

I stopped and took a few deep breaths. I could have gone on for much longer, but the deeper intricacies of spaniel breeding would have been lost on the Sergeant.

'You might not have killed each other, but would you have killed each other's dogs?' he asked.

It was my turn to let amusement show. 'I don't kill dogs,' I said, 'although I can put a dog down if I have to. And she wouldn't kill anything. She preferred to leave the killing to others and keep it out of her woolly mind.' I was not particularly proud of this denigration of the dead, but once the subject of our disagreement had been opened up

I felt determined, against logic and even against my own interests, that the Sergeant should see both sides of the argument.

He looked up from his notebook and raised his eyebrows at me.

'She didn't mind eating meat,' I explained. 'I've seen her tearing into a steak in the hotel's dining room. That, apparently, was different. Training dogs to recover shot game was, in her view, a sin. I, on the other hand, considered her animals to be travesties of what a dog should be, but that doesn't mean that I'd shoot the dog. And I think that that's enough about the difference between my views and those of Mrs Daiches,' I said firmly. 'I did not kill her. I do not kill dogs. I might bomb the Kennel Club some day, though. It's high time we had a separate governing body for gundogs.'

'Now, that's interesting,' the Sergeant said. 'If the Kennel Club goes boom some dark night, I'll come back to you. Why did you say "shoot" the dog? Why not "poison", for instance?'

'We seemed to have been talking about shooting. Any sort of a dog deserves a better death than . . . ' I broke off. 'Mrs Daiches wasn't poisoned, was she?'

'A dog was poisoned, two or three days ago.' He looked at me again sharply, noting my surprise. 'You didn't know?'

'I'm rather off the beaten track for gossip,' I said. 'I tend to catch up with it at irregular intervals, when I walk down to the hotel for a pint.'

He nodded. 'You do seem to live a rather withdrawn life,' he admitted. 'Health, I suppose. No, the dog was poisoned. It was Mrs Daiches who's presumed to have been shot. I expect they'll be . . . examining it later today.' The Sergeant avoided any reference to digging out the bullet, perhaps out of consideration for my presumed delicacy. 'To judge from the entry wound, it was small-bore. A point two-two. You have one of the very few small-bore rifles registered around here,' he finished.

I felt the skin crawl up the back of my neck for an instant. Then I began to get angry. I could think of several others who owned small-bore rifles in the vicinity but I was not going to be the one to name names. For all I knew, some of the weapons might be illegally held. 'I did not shoot Mrs Daiches or anybody else and nor did my rifle,' I said stiffly.

'Shall we take a look at it?'

For my own reasons I would have preferred to put off any such inspection, but a refusal would have looked very suspicious. We walked back to the house, in silence this time. I told myself to stay cool. He was only doing his job. And anger usually left me feeling like hell.

In the recess which formed a sort of back porch, although it was at the front of the house, I turned away from the kitchen and unlocked the door into what had once been a scullery with a small dairy attached.

I saw him stop and look at the lock, which was the only high-security lock in the place. 'There's more money in here than you'd think,' I said. 'This is the shop.'

'Shop?' He sounded doubtful.

The bare, whitewashed room with its few shelves of books and training aids did not look impressive. He seemed to glance around casually without bothering to look. His doubt needled me. 'I found it better to keep a few basics like leads and baskets and bedding for fist-time puppy-buyers, and to sell them some meal to go on with. That saved them having to stop at a pet shop on the way home with a puppy going bonkers in the car. It sort of grew. Now I keep a fairly full selection of training aids and textbooks. And some of the locals buy their dog food from me. It isn't much of an earner but the customers seem to appreciate it.'

He grunted for an answer.

I led him through another door from the shop into my workshop and junk room and unlocked the gun-safe. My one rifle, the old shotgun and an air rifle made a poor showing. Ammunition was stacked on an inner shelf.

'I'll have to take it away,' he said. 'And some cartridges. You'll get it back if it's innocent.'

'It will be,' I said. 'Nobody's been at the gun-safe. You'll give me a proper receipt.' I made it a statement rather than a question.

'Of course. You use it for rabbiting? That's what it says on your certificate.'

'It's the truth,' I told him. 'I defend my vegetable plot, use the shot rabbits for teaching dogs to carry fur, use the skins for training-dummies and boil the meat for adding to the feed. God bless the humble bunny, I say!' I saw no reason to add that I used the rifle most often at dusk and dawn from my bedroom window. This overlooked my vegetable patch but from it I could also see the Daiches' back garden in the distance. Using the telescopic sight as a telescope, I had even watched her fussing with her dogs. I only hoped that nobody had seen me.

The Sergeant stooped to the gun-safe, but it was my shotgun that he drew out. He seemed to have some familiarity with guns, at least to the extent of being able to break it open without fumbling. 'You have a two-two rifle adaptor-tube in the left barrel,' he said sternly.

'I have a two-five blank cartridge adaptor in the left barrel,' I retorted. 'A very different kettle of fish. It's another useful training aid.'

He tried to look through it at the light but, as with the dummy launcher, found that the central hole was in fact two holes at different angles. He closed the shotgun and returned it to the safe. My blank cartridge revolver was on the ammunition shelf. He picked it up, saw that it was exactly what it purported to be and put it back.

My workbench seemed to attract him. He glanced without interest at the accumulation of scraps of pipe and rod and timber under the bench and on the shelves above. I tend to save up the debris of builders and mechanics and as a result can usually find the bits and pieces with which to do small repairs or to improvise training devices simulating the flushing of a bird or rabbit. While he poked through my tools I gave the dummy launcher and its dummies the necessary cleaning before returning them to their place on a high shelf. It was better to be occupied. If I stood idle, I felt that my eyes would be drawn to the one place which I preferred the Sergeant's eyes to avoid. As I fiddled with the cleaning rods and scraps of rag, I turned over in my mind the answers I might give to the question which I was sure was coming.

'What if anything are you looking for?' I asked him. 'Perhaps I can help.'

'A long-series twist drill bit of around seven thirty-seconds of an inch, or perhaps a quarter-inch bit ground down to point two-two.'

'What in hell for?' Perhaps it was slow of me. If so, blame that damned, eternal tiredness.

'That dummy launcher has all the makings of a straightened-out two-two pistol,' he said, watching my face. 'We have to consider whether somebody, not necessarily yourself, might not have taken one and bored the central hole through to the end. Nobody around here would think twice if another person walked around with a dummy launcher. But your drill-bits are all too short for the job.'

I leaned against the bench while I thought about it. My legs were beginning to shake. 'I suppose it might work,' I said at last. 'But you'd still have the problem of another hole going off at an angle. It'd be dangerous. And hellish inaccurate. It would kick to one side.' As I was speaking, it occurred to me that it would be much easier and more effective to drill a larger hole back from the solid end to meet the others, but the Sergeant was already overfull of ideas.

'If somebody came up close— ' he began.

'Why on earth go to all that trouble, bugger up an expensive device and leave a lot of permanent evidence behind? A firearm is for striking from a distance. If somebody could come close enough to shoot her with something so primitive, they might just as well bonk her on the head.'

He was not one to give up easily. 'How many launchers do you have in use?' he asked.

'Just the one. There should be three or four more in the shop.'

'There are three,' he said without taking his eyes off me. So he had been taking notice after all. 'Still in the manufacturer's packaging.'

'So you'd better look somewhere else.'

'I will,' he said. 'Of course, a firearm isn't only used to attack from a distance. It also enables the weak to overcome the strong. You used to have a couple of two-two pistols on your certificate. You're sure you got rid of them?'

'Quite sure. I sold them when I left the rifle and pistol club and I can refer you to the dealer who bought them.'

He collected my rifle and samples of various types of ammunition – high-velocity for accuracy at a distance and subsonic for when a quieter shot was needed. I was relieved to follow him out and lock the door. He said that he would be looking around the garden for a while and I told him to go ahead but not to aggravate the dogs. It only occurred to me later, when the blanket of exhaustion fell over me again, that he had been watching me for a reaction when he spoke about the weak overcoming the strong. The thought both angered and amused me. I might not be the man that once I had been. The Sergeant could have overcome me with ease. But I would have matched myself against the late Mrs Daiches almost any day of the week, two falls or submissions or one knockout to decide the winner.

Sergeant Flodden seemed to be pottering aimlessly around the garden and poking into the outbuildings. I guessed that he had decided to take no positive action while I was watching him. Perversely, I was still keeping an eye on him when a mud-encrusted Land-Rover rumbled up to the door and disgorged Andrew Williamson.

Andrew had made an excellent job of grassing over the site of the now defunct buildings, although at a less than excellent price, but that did not make him one of my favourite people. The farm which he rented had absorbed its neighbours several years earlier so that from a farmhouse and steading near the village he farmed most of the land thereabouts. He struck me as not very bright – a good enough farmer although always short of capital and usually a few years behind the times. Sometimes it was hard to tell where his midden ended and the farmyard began. He was a lean, dark man in his forties with a perpetually disgruntled expression and he descended to the ground as though he were going into battle. But that was just his way. He had probably emerged into the world with his little fists clenched.

'I'm needing all-in-one meal,' he said. 'Just a wee puckle to tide me over. Say twa pun'. I'll get more in Cupar, the morn. Yours is o'er dear.' Nobody would ever have described him as gracious.

The feed room was a former larder off the big kitchen. While I weighed some meal into a paper bag he took root in one of the fireside chairs. His boots and dungarees were foul. Beth would have had him out of there in a minute, but she was not there to object and I could not be bothered. There would, I thought, be some other reason for his visit. His two collies were usually fed on scraps.

'You heard about yon wifie Daiches?' he asked when I returned.

'Just now,' I said. 'A police sergeant told me. He took away my two-two rifle.'

'They took mine and a'. I telled them to be damned quick. I askit them what I was to do if another dog came chasing my ewes. They couldna' tell me.' But Andrew had not come to discuss firearms. He went off at a tangent. 'You're still takin' your dogs on my land.'

I sat down opposite him. 'It's not your land,' I told him patiently for perhaps the hundredth time. 'It's Lord Craill's

68

land and I have his written permission to train dogs on it. And to shoot over it.'

'It's easy enough for him to hand out permits. He doesna' hae tae thole the parasites dogs can carry— '

'Rubbish!' I said. I keep my dogs well wormed. And although dogs pick up sheep ticks I never heard of a sheep picking up a dog tick.

' — nor the disturbance to the sheep. And nothing in it for myself.'

'There's a bottle of whisky in it for you at Christmas,' I reminded him, 'which is something for nothing as far as you're concerned. Do you remember the time a whole lot of lambs got out of your paddock? I was passing with two of my dogs and you asked me to use them to keep the lambs back from the road while your collies gathered them.'

'Aye. And a pig's arse they made of it,' he said triumphantly.

'That's because I walk dogs at heel through sheep until they ignore them. I teach them that sheep aren't real. My dogs thought that your lambs were figments of their imaginations. And the lambs knew it and didn't pay the dogs a damn bit of notice. That's why I couldn't get them to work properly. If any dog from here ever chases your sheep it'll be a young puppy not trained yet. Just come and tell me.'

'When it happens, I'll shoot the bugger,' he said.

I kept hold of my temper although the day was testing it severely. Dr Harper was always lecturing me about the avoidance of stress. And this was not the time for an exchange of threats involving firearms. 'Not without having another lawsuit on your hands you won't,' I said. 'I thought you'd have had enough of lawyers by now.'

'By God I have! But yon old biddy being dead, that should change things.'

The lawsuit over the death of Mrs Cory's valuable brood bitch and a counter-suit over two ewes which had allegedly miscarried had been wandering ever since around the corridors of the law and was only now about to come to court.

'Now it's just her word against yours,' I said. 'Unless Mrs Daiches left a sworn statement?'

His expression flickered. 'If she did, she'll not be there to back it up. And I've you for a sichter.'

A sichter is a witness. 'For the umpteenth time, Andrew,' I said, 'I saw nothing. When I arrived on the scene, the dog was dead or dying and you and those two harpies were slanging at each other.'

'You saw blood on the tyke's jaws.'

'I did. But you'd just shot it through the lungs. I saw no blood on any of your sheep.'

'You could ha' done.' His face bore an insinuating smirk and his eyes were trying to send a message.

'Easily,' I said. 'That older collie of yours isn't above giving the sheep a nip if they won't move as he wants them. Andrew, I am not going to commit perjury for you or for anybody else. If anyone's daft enough to call me, I'll tell the truth as I saw it, which was bloody little, and that's the end.'

'It'll not be the end of it.' He got up and walked out of the house. I followed him, for the pleasure of watching him go. 'I'm the wrong man to cross,' he said as he unlocked the Land-Rover. 'And it's not as if it'd mak' any odds. The courts aye believe the farmer.'

I was not so sure that he was right. Courts will believe the worst of any dog from a fighting strain. But they think that they know about spaniels.

'If you think that,' I said, 'stop bugging me.'

He drove off, first reversing onto the grass and making a scar which would remain until the spring. He had not offered to pay for the dogfood but I was too relieved to see the back of him to care.

# SEVEN

Isobel and Beth, when they were away, never expected me to do more than keep the dogs cleaned and fed. Usually I tried to do more, but lassitude and circumstances were conspiring against me that day. I toyed with another snack and took a short rest. Even my rest was spoiled by two phone calls which fetched me out of my chair and through to the small office. One was from a client, the other from a vet on the RCVS Eye Panel with some data for Isobel's compulsive accumulation of facts. I spent ten minutes, irritably jotting down details of pedigrees.

The dogs were restless, trying to remind me that it was dinner-time. Sergeant Flodden had vanished or I would have put him to work again. I gave the dogs their main meal and let them out, one group at a time, to make use of the grass while I cleaned the pens and at the same time tried to maintain discipline and even to reinforce the lessons already learned. Sitting at a distance and coming quickly to the whistle can never be too deeply impressed on the canine mind which is largely governed by habit – its dominant thought being 'This is how we always do it'. More intensive training could wait until the Monday when we would be back to full strength.

The light was going. The field trial would be over. I made a cup of weak tea and stayed within hearing distance of the phone.

Something was nagging at me. I should have faced up to it before, but I knew that, ostrich-like, I had been burying my mind in the sand. It was something which I had seen while I was with the Sergeant. Or, to be more exact, something which I had expected to see when I looked for it out of the corner of my eye. I unlocked the shop and went through into the workshop to look on a high shelf. But there was nothing there. I looked on other shelves and then went through the whole of the untidy room, but what I wanted had gone. I locked up again, carefully, telling myself things about stable doors.

I was sitting and miserably chewing on the problem when the phone went. I dragged myself through to the small office and answered it. Beth's clear, young voice came on the line, driving all thoughts of murder out of my head. I could hear chatter in the background.

'Mr Cunningham?'

'Speaking, Beth. How did we get on?'

'We got second, and a couple of minor awards.' There was a great happiness in her voice. Beth cared how the dogs got on just as much as Isobel or I did.

'That's wonderful,' I said. 'Taken with the first he got at Amulree, he qualifies for the Championship Trial. We'll make him up yet.'

'We were lucky. He wiped Featherstone Juliet's eye on a long runner and pushed her into third. I'm not even sure that it was the same bird. And Hargrove Bertie was put out for being hardmouthed although the pheasant came down stone dead from about a hundred feet up. I reckon it landed on a stone.' The more important topic being covered, Beth's voice sobered suddenly. 'You heard about Mrs Daiches?'

'Yes. I've had the police around the place. How did you hear?'

'Somebody at the trial got word and spoke to Mrs Kitts. I'm afraid she's . . . '

'Celebrating her victory? Or holding a wake?' I finished for her. 'Give her my congratulations.'

'Yes, of course I will. I think she looks on it as a double

celebration,' Beth said. 'She didn't like Mrs Daiches any more than you did, or me, or anybody. She's on top of the world but I think I can get her away soon. You're going to have to work hard tonight, I'm afraid. I'll take her straight home if I can.'

'Try very hard,' I said.

When we had disconnected, I sat and did some more thinking. Beth had made an odd choice of words. I had taken Isobel Kitts as a partner because of her qualification as a vet and because I needed additional capital. She had gained some experience as a picker-up when her husband had been active in the gundog field. But that she had turned out to be a brilliant dog-handler had been an enormous and unexpected bonus.

But there were drawbacks. The drinking was now occasional and seemed to be confined to special occasions. It was worth losing Beth's help around the place for a day to ensure that Isobel and the dog both returned safely. By next morning, Isobel would be ready to face anything except loud noises. But she was inclined to return from her forays in amorous mood.

When Isobel had given up veterinary practice it had been to marry a man substantially older than herself. I had come to like Henry very much.

The marriage had worn well. They enjoyed a sociable drink together although I would not have cared to guess which one of them had led the other into the habit. Unusually but wisely, when they were out together they never drank simultaneously to excess. Henry Kitts was now well past sixty and, according to hints dropped by Isobel, was no longer the demon lover that, again according to Isobel, he had once been.

On several occasions since the night of Isobel's first triumph, I had been called on to deputise for Henry and I had never found a formula for refusing such an offer without giving offence to a well-liked and much-valued partner. She was a well-preserved forty and stripped well, but she would not have been my choice of a paramour. I was fond of Isobel, and her attitude to me, even in bed, was still motherly. Her embraces were no great hardship but, frankly, I found them rather hard work. On such occasions, Isobel had been known to remark out of the blue that she had decided not to leave Henry for me – not that I had ever asked her to do so. But on those occasions she had invariably been in her cups and I thought and hoped that she was never likely to change her mind.

Beth, who must have been well aware of the liaison and seemed much amused by it, had said that I was going to have to 'work hard tonight'. Had she meant that I would have to work hard to avoid Isobel's clutches? Or in them? No, surely not that. Beth seemed too innocent for such an innuendo, but perhaps that was an illusion deriving from her apparent youth. I had noticed before that most people, even the most modest of maiden ladies, once they involved themselves with the breeding of animals soon adopted a down-to-earth attitude to the process of procreation.

The house seemed very silent and lonely. I visited the kennels and took two of the youngsters into the barn. But my mind was not on their training and the dogs knew it and started to play me up. I put them firmly through a couple of simple exercises – as I had told the Sergeant, you must always finish on a triumph, never on a failure – and shut them away again.

Rather than sit alone, I decided to go down to the hotel and see what I could learn. I locked up the kennels. There is no way to make a wire mesh run secure against a determined thief, but I had my own methods. Two microphones were concealed in the structure of the kennels and relayed any sounds from the dogs through loudspeakers in the house. In the hall, I switched on a Citizens' Band transmitter which was linked to the same system. If any stranger approached the house or kennels, the dogs would let me know. When I tested the pocket receiver I could hear one of the dogs yipping as it chased rabbits in its sleep. The chasing of rabbits is taboo, except only in dreams.

Beth and Mrs Kitts had my car. It was time the business had a second car or a van. I walked. I could have gone by the road, but it was narrow and the thorn hedges were uncomfortably close to the verge if a vehicle should come along. Instead, I took a field path which led me behind Mrs Cory's house. One of her dogs started barking its silly head off, but that was her problem and not mine. The night was clear and frosty but calm – good weather for stretching the legs and breathing the cold air.

A few yards further on, my path brought me out between two gables into the village street. Should I call on Jim Daiches, I wondered? To offer him commiseration when I felt no misery would be the kind of hypocrisy which I deplore, on a par with praying, when in trouble, to a God who has been forgotten in the good times. The passing of his wife would be no more to me than a temporary nuisance and a permanent relief. Condolences, perhaps, I could offer. But, judging from the activity around his house and the caravan, he would still have police in the house and neighbours fussing round. The vitriolic Mrs Cory lived opposite and if she could be said to have a soft spot for any human being it was certainly for her friend's husband.

I walked on and turned in at the doors of the hotel.

For a small village, we were blessed with a hotel which was further upmarket than we had any right to expect. The local hotel had begun its life as a coaching inn. Much later, when road widening and straightening works some miles away had led most of the traffic onto an easier route, the inn might have degenerated into a local boozer.

But the management of the time had been more far-seeing. Instead of allowing business to contract, they had forcefully expanded it by arranging fishing holidays and

other sporting occasions and by maintaining and adver-
tising a cuisine which now brought travellers from as far as
Perth or Kirkcaldy or Edinburgh. Honeymooners and dirty
weekenders came from even farther afield. Locally, lacking
any other gathering point except for a small and draughty
church hall, it functioned as the hub of all socialising. Even
the Springs, who were staunch teetotallers, were welcome
to sit over a gossip and tomato juice for a whole evening
at a time.

The big bar was remarkably full even for a Saturday
night. A tangy smell of woodsmoke, which I always suspected of having arrived by aerosol despite the existence
of an open fireplace, fought with tobacco smoke and the
smell of drink. The Muzak was almost inaudible behind
the chatter. There were some familiar faces. Of the others,
it was difficult to distinguish between reporters, curious
sensation-seekers and policemen temporarily off duty. As
much of the floor as was not taken up by human feet was
occupied by dogs of all varieties. For them, it was a perfect
environment for exchanging fleas, diseases and bad habits,
which was why I so rarely brought any of my own for
company and the exercise.

Neill Cory was at the bar. Much as I had disliked the
two lady spaniel breeders I had always got on well with
their husbands, so I pushed my way towards him.

Laurie Duffus intercepted me. His triangular face with
its drooping moustache was flushed and his eyes glittered.
I could see that he had passed beyond his point of no return.
A harmless enough character when sober or only mildly
drunk, Laurie was one of those regrettable drinkers who,
once a certain point had been passed, become quarrelsome.
Laurie's commitment at the local market garden varied
with the seasons so he was in the habit of supplementing
his income by taking casual work when the market garden
was slack. I guessed that he would now be employed
on gritting the roads. He kept two Labradors, trained
them himself and defended the market garden against the

depredations of rabbits by shooting over the dogs, but his entries in retriever trials were limited by the availability of time and cash.

He grabbed my arm or I would have passed by with a nod. 'You heard about Madam Daiches,' he said. It was a statement rather than a question.

'I heard,' I said.

'Who you think killed her?' He squinted at me. He was further gone than I had thought. ''Twasn't me. Was it you?'

I tried to escape his grip but it was impossible without using enough force to provoke a fight. 'What on earth would I want to do that for?' I asked.

'You couldn't abide the woman,' he said. 'Well, no more could I. But I had good reason. Had to put up with her living next door, didn't I? You think she was easy to live next door to?'

I kept my voice as low as was possible while still being heard. 'I'd forgotten that she was your neighbour. She must have been— ' I nearly said murder ' — hell to live near.'

'You're right. But you didn' have to. My guess is, you were jealous. Her dogs were prettier than yours. Tha's what spaniels are. Pretty dogs. Hers could've beaten yours out of sight in a trial.'

'You're out of your mind,' I said, laughing. 'You'd better let me see you home before you end up inside the bottle. You're just narked because I put you out of a trial when your dog ran in to shot. He took off after a rabbit— '

'It'd been pricked, I swear it!' For a moment his voice stilled the hubbub in the room. Dogs can arouse grander passions than love. 'A retriever's s'posed to retrieve what's shot, yes? 'Sall right for you. Spaniels only have to rampage around the bushes, scaring out anything that's stupid enough to pay any attention to them. They can't retrieve worth a damn anyway.'

I stopped laughing. This was fighting talk. 'Tell you

what I'll do,' I said. 'I'll put up one of my spaniels against either of your Labs in a straight retrieving test, for a hundred quid. Are you on?' I looked around. 'We'll need witnesses . . . '

He was far gone but not as far gone as that. He shook his head as if to clear it and let go of my arm.

'Any time you change your mind,' I said. I moved on, smiling. Laurie had handed me the perfect means of sending him on his way whenever he was in his obstreperous mood.

I squeezed my way to the bar and tried to get the barmaid's attention. A hand caught my elbow and a voice said 'Pint of Guinness is it?'

I nodded. It was easier than shouting. I had been thinking along the lines of a double brandy, but decided against it. At a time of ill-health it is all too easy to slip into a habit of heavy drinking.

Henry Kitts caught the barmaid's eye – which was more than I had managed to do, but he topped me by several inches and his hooked nose and high colour took nothing away from a commanding presence. 'Don't know how you manage to drink that stuff,' he said.

'I don't either,' I said. 'I'm only now beginning to acquire the taste. It just makes all other beers taste like piss. Dr Harvey says it might help me to put some weight back on.'

He looked at me critically. 'It hasn't done much for you so far,' he said. The Guinness arrived. 'Let's find a quiet corner.'

There were no seats to be had. We tucked ourselves into a nook at the extreme end of the bar. I still had to speak up but I had no problem in hearing. Henry, like many an older man whose hearing has begun to fail, had developed a loud voice. I expected him to talk about the murder but, as with Beth, first things came first. 'I hear you got a second,' he said. 'Isobel phoned me. So now you can go for gold, try for the championship, eh?'

'That's the general idea. And if anybody can do it, Isobel can.'

'I believe you, my boy. Look how she makes me jump through hoops.' He beamed at me. Although he was twice my age, he had twice the vitality. 'You heard about Laura Daiches?'

'There was a police sergeant at me for half the day,' I said. 'I had to cut out most of my training schedule. Although, to be fair, he did help with feeding the pups. He took away my two-two rifle. I gather that Mrs Daiches was killed by something similar.'

'An easy day now and again won't do the dogs any harm.' Henry had been a noted handler in his day and still kept an old spaniel. 'But if your sergeant told you that Laura Daiches was shot to death, he lied.'

'I don't think he said quite that. Should we be talking like this in here?' I added.

He glanced around at the crowd, which was slowly thinning as those who had not yet eaten drifted home or into the dining room. 'What the hell do you think they're all talking about?'

'True. The Sergeant told me that she seemed to have a bullet in her.'

'Not quite the same thing. And also not quite true. She died from strangulation. Hugh Miller found her – the milkman, you know him?'

'Only to shout at when he makes too much noise in the morning and sets the dogs barking.' I took a pull at my Guinness and found that I was beginning to like it.

'He didn't tell me anything about a bullet,' Henry said resentfully. He led a quiet life and hated to be left off the grapevine. 'I only found out about it later. But Hugh said that her coat was powdered with frost when he found her, so maybe he didn't see it. He usually leaves her milk at the front. But he got there before dawn, which is how he came to notice that the light over the back door was still on. And her dogs were kicking up a fuss, so he took a look. It must have given him a hell of a shock. He said that her silk scarf had been pulled very tightly round her neck and knotted. But even if he hadn't seen the scarf, he said that he'd have known from the face.'

I preferred to avoid speaking, or even thinking, about the face of someone who had died in that way. 'It all sounds very hard to believe,' I said. 'Even when you've accepted the fact of a woman being deliberately killed in our peaceful corner – where the apex of drama is usually two dogs fighting over a bone – the idea that she was killed by two different methods is weird. Unless . . . from what the Sergeant told me, all they knew at the time was that she seemed to have a bullet-hole in her. Could somebody have strangled her and then, not being sure that she was dead, stabbed her with some sort of spike?'

'Ingenious,' Henry said, 'but no. I must have been visited later than you. By an inspector and a constable,' he added, as though that put him one up on me. 'Somebody seems to have told them that I had a small-bore rifle but I haven't. Gave it up years ago. I said that their informant, whom they refused to name – assuming, I suppose, that we would never guess who it was – must have seen me with the airgun I use on the starlings and not known the difference. Anyway, they were still waiting for the pathologist to do his stuff but they were quite definite. Hole clean through the body. And not in anything like a straight line. Got to have been a bullet.'

'Then it doesn't make sense.'

'It could do.' Henry was an avid reader of mysteries and claimed always to arrive at a solution before the fictional detective, if the writer had played fair. 'I think you were looking at it the wrong way round. The killer is somebody who'd threatened her, or who she was scared of for some other reason. She'd have screamed her head off if he'd come any closer. So he . . . or she . . . let's call it "they" . . . they shoot her from over the garden fence. A two-two bullet's very small and doesn't pack much of a punch but it could go right through if it didn't hit a major bone. She goes down but she's obviously far from dead. So he hops over the fence or goes round by that gate at the corner of the garden and finishes her off with her scarf.'

'Why not another bullet?' For the tenth time, I put the little radio to my ear. One of the dogs was snoring. I recognised Hector of Bravington's snore, which had the high-pitched drone of a model aeroplane.

'I can think of a dozen reasons,' Henry said. 'A two-two isn't very loud. The neighbours might well put one shot down to somebody doing a little late training with a blank cartridge pistol. But it would have set her stupid beasts barking. Imagine her husband or a neighbour sticking their head out of the window and saying, "What's all the row about?" '

'I suppose it could have happened that way,' I said.

'That or about ten others.'

'Were any shots heard?'

'That, of course, is the question they're all asking each other. Since nobody, not even the police, has much idea of the time of death yet, their answers don't mean very much. From what I could learn before you came in, somebody was banging away up at your place just after dusk. And some-body else – probably Neill Cory – was flighting pigeon in the big wood. I haven't heard of any other shots. Not yet. But there was some hammering going on.'

'I was doing some pup-training in the barn, using blanks.'

Henry looked at me with mild anxiety. 'I hope you can prove it if you have to. Your regular shouting matches with the late lady must put you fairly high on the list of suspects. And while we're on the subject of your activities,' he added, 'I knew there was something else I meant to ask you. Are you sleeping with my wife?'

Was it imagination or had conversation in the bar faltered for a second? I forced myself to look around. Nobody seemed to be looking our way. Or were they avoiding my eye? There were no notebooks to be seen.

'It's all right,' Henry said. 'They're talking murder. In fact, this is probably the first evening for months they're not talking about you two. It's all right,' he repeated. 'I don't mind. Twenty years ago, ten even, I'd have minded like hell; but I'm getting past that sort of thing now. Sex, I mean. Frankly, when you come to my age you'll find that it isn't worth the effort. You begin to wonder what all the fuss was about.'

'For Christ's sake, Henry,' I began.

He rolled on without hearing me. 'So what I wanted to say was that, if you are, for God's sake be a man and make a proper job of it. An upstanding young fellow like you, even if you are a bit underweight, shouldn't be sending her home to me still expecting attention I'm no longer fit to provide. And I don't want her getting discontented again and wandering off in search of a bit of rough. I'd hate that.' His voice seemed to rebound from the high ceiling. He was warming to his theme. 'Getting an Argie bullet through you is no excuse. They didn't shoot your balls off, did they?'

'I did not stop a bullet in the . . . the Falklands,' I said firmly. It felt strange to be apologising to a husband for not being fit enough to service his wife more thoroughly but I felt that I had to make the effort. 'I came through without a scratch and then picked up a bug in Central America—'

'Lower your voice,' he said sternly. 'Here they come.'

Beth seemed to arrive first bounce. She was in her early twenties but I still had to make the effort to remember that she was not a schoolgirl – she seemed the very personification of youth with her long-legged walk, short skirts, anoraks and sensible shoes. Her face, too, showed off a perfect complexion and big, bright eyes. Her dark hair was pulled back into a pony-tail. I was not alone in my difficulty. Policemen were always checking her driving licence in the belief that she must be under-age.

'We thought you'd be here. Isn't it great?' she said. 'Can

we still get an entry for the Spaniel Championship Stake? Could I have a shandy, please?'

Taking her questions in order I said that it was, that there were places reserved for late qualifiers and that she certainly could. 'What's Isobel drinking?' I asked.

'Brandy and soda. Have you been all right?'

I sighed. Brandy always seemed to inflame the passionate side of Isobel's nature. 'I've been fine. You'll have the other half?' I asked Henry.

'Pint of Eighty Shilling,' he said after careful deliberation, although he rarely drank anything else except when he was heading for a real binge. Only a weak bladder and a great deal of walking saved him from developing a beer-belly.

The order was waiting on the bar long before Isobel reached us. She had paused for a word with Mr McCready, our local vet. Their relationship had never been of the best. Mr McCready was an elderly man, ostensibly in semi-retirement, but he still expected to do all the veterinary work in the neighbourhood. Isobel, who wanted no more than to concentrate on Three Oaks Kennels and to exercise her skills on the minor ailments of our residents and the relentless tracking of congenital ailments through pedigrees, would have been happy to leave the rest to him. Unfortunately his manner was so unpleasant, and his reputation so much damaged by persistent rumours, that animal owners preferred to call on her for help. Isobel tried hard to remain within the bounds of professional etiquette, but not always to the satisfaction of Mr McCready.

Their voices were rising above the hubbub in the bar.

'I certainly did try to contact you,' Isobel was saying. 'Either you were out or you were asleep.'

'It could have waited,' McCready retorted. He had a penetrating, nasal voice which dominated the room. The plaintive note was unmistakable.

'No way could it have waited. It was an emergency. And the owner had already made up his mind to drive the poor creature into St Andrews if I wouldn't act.'

83

(She was letting him down lightly. I had overheard the distraught owner's words. 'I wouldn't go back to that fool McCready for a flea-powder,' had been the kindest of them.)

Beth was speaking to me. 'Who on earth could have done such a thing to Mrs Daiches?' she asked.

'Henry can tell you all about it,' I said.

I had missed the first part of McCready's retort. ' . . . after that flagrant piece of poaching you come to me for help?'

Isobel's voice was slightly slurred but she spoke slowly and lucidly. She was never an aggressive drunk. 'I'm not equipped for major surgery and I prefer never to operate on my husband's bitch. Liza's hormones are playing up and it's time she was spayed.'

Firmly bypassing the point, McCready said, 'Somebody's been spreading rumours about me.' (This was true. Mrs Cory had been damning him from here to breakfast time.)

'Not me,' Isobel said. 'And as far as I'm concerned, you're competent until you prove yourself otherwise. Do the job or turn it down, it's all the same to me.'

They spoke, in calmer tones, for another minute or two before Isobel broke away and joined us. She was walking with care but otherwise you would never have known that her bloodstream was ninety proof.

'Silly man!' she said. 'He couldn't see that I was only trying to do him a favour. Asking him, in the middle of a crowd, if he'd operate on poor old Liza seemed the best way of countering the poison that Mrs Cory's been spreading about him. He's competent enough; it's his manner that makes him enemies. And he's trying to pretend that he's broken-hearted over Mrs Daiches. Only a week ago he was calling her a fool and a crook for backing up Olive Cory over a valuation. As the Americans say, he can dish it out but he can't take it.'

Isobel was, as I have said, well preserved. Even seen beside Beth she could have passed for thirty. Her Wellingtons had been changed for court shoes and she had disposed of the old waterproof which she would have worn at the Field Trial. Her soft tweeds were definitely for the country but, with her hair plainly but skilfully dressed, she looked as if she had dressed for a party. She was plump but in a firm, bouncy style that promised – and provided – greater delights than any fashionable slimness.

'Many congratulations,' I said. 'Here's a drink in celebration. If you'd got another first, he'd have been a Field Trial Champion and it would have been champagne.'

She accepted the brandy. 'Remind me to get a first next time,' she said. 'We were unlucky.'

'Luck always comes into it, no matter how hard the judges try to be fair,' I said. 'Just be luckier at the Spaniel Championship Stake. A good placing there brings more kudos, and opens more purse-strings, than a title gained over two lesser events. But you'll make it. You're the best handler in the business.'

'Dear boy!' she said, smiling. 'Never stop telling me that.'

All Beth's attention had seemed to be on the details of the murder which Henry was shouting into her ear, but she had heard our exchange. 'You don't think that Mr Cunningham's training might have had something to do with it?' she asked. It was as near as I ever heard her come to being catty.

Isobel's lip twitched. I thought that she was going to snap out a tart reply. Then she relaxed visibly. 'It had everything to do with it,' she said. She stretched to kiss me on the cheek and whispered in my ear. 'I think you deserve a little tender, loving care.'

So Beth had been right. Isobel was feeling amorous. I tried, unsuccessfully, to think of a polite evasion. I was saved by what I thought at the time to be a happy coincidence. The small radio which I was still holding began to bark its head off. Henry spluttered into his beer and Beth jumped like a startled faun.

'I'll go,' I said quickly. 'It's probably only the police sniffing around. But I heard something about dog-poisoning. The car's at the front?'

'Yes,' Beth said. 'But I'll come— '

'I'll be back,' I said. 'Stay and enjoy your drinks. It may only be a fox.'

I got out into the chill, fresh air.

In good health, I could have run the distance to the kennels in a few minutes, but not in my debilitated state. The large estate car was parked a few yards along the kerb. I dug out my own key. Samson snuffled as I got in. He was a wise and experienced little dog and he knew from the reactions of Isobel and Beth that he had done well. He expected a few moments of petting but he had to make do with a quick word of greeting. I was in a hurry.

The moon was up and I knew the road well. I could manage without lights. Rather than arrive noisily, I spurted up to forty, switched off and coasted the slight upward gradient. The car came to a halt near the gates.

I got out quietly, easing the car door shut, and hurried over the grass. My warm coat was still hanging in the bar and I felt the cold biting even through my thickest sweater and the scarf which was tucked into it. I had left the lights on over the kennels and runs and there was nobody to be seen there. At my approach the last of the barking stopped.

The house looked normal but I headed for the back door to make a quick check. I had the house keys in my hand as I stepped into the dark recess.

Something hard hit me in the stomach. It was a blow which should not have bothered me but I went down as if I had stopped the bullet with which my friends were determined to credit me.

Feet gritted on the gravel and somebody stooped over me. Hands took hold of my scarf, pulled the knot round to the back and jerked it tight.

I blacked out. It was just like falling asleep.

# EIGHT

I came round as suddenly and as completely as I had blacked out. This, I was told later, was typical of unconsciousness produced by cutting off the blood supply to the brain for a short period. Apart from a soreness around the solar plexus, I felt quite up to my usual, not very high, standard. Even my brain, which too often felt as if it were coated in treacle, was clear. The bright light which was bothering my eyes turned out to be the lamp over the back door which somebody had switched on. The face of Henry, dramatically side-lit, was looking anxiously down on me. My head was in a comfortable lap which turned out to be Beth's.

'Was the scarf still tied round my neck when you got here?' I asked. It seemed a reasonable question. My last conscious thought had been to wonder whether I was being murdered or if this was a mere assault.

Henry looked surprised but Beth was quite matter-of-fact. 'It was on the ground,' she said.

'But are you all right?' Henry asked.

'We followed you up in Henry's car almost straight away,' Beth said. 'We've only just got here. How do you feel? Do you want a doctor?' She seemed not to have grasped the purpose of my question but she had told me what I wanted to know.

Footsteps came hurrying from the direction of the kennels and Isobel's face appeared. 'The dogs are all right,' she said. 'How about you?'

'Just a bit shaky. And bloody cold. I'll be all right,' I said, answering all three enquiries together. Beth helped me up. I was about to confirm my wellbeing when I realised that I had been handed, on a plate, the perfect excuse. ' — in the morning,' I added quickly. 'I think I'd be better for a quiet lie down.'

It was Henry who looked disappointed. Isobel took my dereliction philosophically. 'That would be best,' she said. 'They weren't after the dogs, were they?'

'Not this time,' I said. It had been the fear of dognapping which had provoked us into providing the microphones. Good working dogs can be valuable even without the pedigrees. And owners of bitches have even been known to steal the service of a good stud-dog. 'They seemed to be trying for the house.'

'It was still locked up,' Beth said. 'But your keys were lying on the ground beside you. Shall I call the police?' Her voice was beginning to tremble now that the emergency was over.

'Let's see whether we've lost anything first,' I said. I faced Henry and Isobel. 'Thanks for coming to the rescue. I'll be grateful if you don't say anything about this to anybody.'

'I hope you know what you're doing,' Isobel said. 'Henry says that Laura Daiches was strangled with a scarf.'

'Which may have put the idea into somebody else's mind,' I said. 'The murderer would have left it knotted. So please, say nothing.'

'I have no intention of putting the thought of robbing this place into anybody else's head,' Isobel said. She swayed and leaned on Henry's arm. 'Come, darling. It's nearly our bed-time.'

'My coat's still hanging in the bar,' I said. 'Would you collect it for me, please?'

Henry gave me a reproachful look and led Isobel back towards his car.

'That was naughty,' Beth said. 'You are all right really?'

'I'm fine. I just didn't fancy having Isobel hanging round any longer.'

'You just didn't fancy having Mrs Kitts,' Beth said with more accuracy than tact.

'Beth,' I said, 'I don't think you should speak like that. Whatever you know and whatever you think.'

She looked down. 'I'm sorry,' she said. 'Truly. And now I'm going to see for myself that the dogs are all right. Mrs Kitts didn't spend seconds with them, she was in too much of a hurry to get back to you. Do you feel up to bringing the car in and letting Samson out of his box?'

'Right,' I said.

'You don't think that the . . . burglar, or whatever he was, is still hanging around?'

'If he wanted something, he probably got it,' I said. 'But if you see any shadows move, scream like hell.'

'Don't think I wouldn't.' Her voice held a shiver.

We met again outside the run which adjoined Samson's kennel. I made a special fuss of him and put him inside, together with the private bowl, bearing his name in large letters, from which he insisted on taking his food and water. Samson was always the prima donna of the kennels. 'Presumably he's been fed,' I said.

Beth did not bother to answer, treating my words as no more than a statement of the obvious. When a dog went away, she took the necessary number of prepared meals along. 'Presumably you haven't,' she said.

'I seem to have been eating all day.'

'Two cups of coffee and a sweet biscuit. I know you. And you must be freezing. Come along.' She took my arm and almost pulled me towards the house. 'I like Mrs Kitts,' she said unhappily. 'I really do. She's a nice person. I don't even mind her taking a dram now and again, 'specially as it gets me a chance to go to the trials with her. It just narks me that she expects you to jump into bed with her whenever she feels like it. She thinks that she's doing you a favour, and she can't see that you dread it but are

89

too polite to say so. So I've said it and now I'll never say another word, I promise.'

The subject seemed to be closed, and better so. I wanted to go into the shop but she dragged me into the kitchen and pushed me into a chair and I had neither the energy nor the willpower to resist. The kitchen was warm from the central heating boiler and I felt the chill seeping away.

'I thought as much,' she said over her shoulder from the fridge. 'The steak pie that I left for you has hardly been touched. By my reckoning you've had two fish fingers and an egg in the last twenty-four hours.'

'Plus at least two sandwiches and a pint of Guinness,' I said.

She humphed and went on scolding me while she did things with the microwave. Usually a reticent person, she could become garrulous only about the progress of the dogs and quite bossy when it came to matters which she thought affected my health. And although she was an obedient and almost deferential employee about the kennels, in the house she seemed to have appointed herself, as had Isobel, a sort of honorary matriarch. When she had first accepted the post, the arrangement had been that a flatlet would be carved out of the upstairs for her; but long before the alterations could be put in hand Beth had been using my bathroom and had taken over the kitchen. She had a bedroom to herself and in theory a small sitting room, but when we had time to sit we both usually sat in the large kitchen which contained, in addition to all the usual equipment, two fireside chairs and a seldom-used television. I suspected that Henry was wrong. If the local gossips credited me with a mistress, Beth's name was more likely to have been on their tongues than Isobel's.

By a mixture of bullying and charm, Beth could usually coerce me into having an appetite. By the time that she put the steak pie and some vegetables on the table I was almost hungry. As we ate, Beth gave me a minute-by-minute account of the day. Samson, it seemed, had started off over-eager and determined to quest too quickly and too far ahead, but Isobel had soon reminded him who was the leader of the pack. He settled down and his game-finding and retrieving had both been impeccable. At one point there were two birds down, both dead, but the judge wanted Isobel to send him to gather them in the order in which they had been shot.

'But,' Beth said, 'the second bird was near him and in the open and that was the one he was determined to go for.'

'It would be,' I said.

'Mrs Kitts sent him towards the other one, but he did a quick U-turn and she was only just quick enough to stop him on the whistle, three or four yards from the wrong bird. What would you have done?'

'Panicked, probably.'

Beth looked at me curiously. 'I don't think you would. But Mrs Kitts stayed absolutely calm. She whistled him towards her and sat him again. He was still turning his head to look at the bird in the open. She called him a little bit closer twice more and made him sit and wait until he seemed to be forgetting about that bird. Then she gave him a very firm signal to go out the other way. And from there on he was perfect. The judge looked quite pleased.'

I found that I was holding my breath as Beth described this near-disaster. Her word picture was so graphic that I could visualise the scene as though I were there. When she finished, I was surprised to find that I had eaten my share of the steak pie, an apple and some biscuits and cheese and felt much better for it.

My physical malaise might have lessened but the worry was still there.

'Won't you tell me what's bothering you?' Beth said. 'It isn't just the murder of somebody none of us liked very much.' She paused and made a face. 'Well, we didn't and there's no point pretending. And if we had a burglar, he doesn't seem to have taken anything.'

Although we had been living at close quarters for more than a year, I had never got into the habit of confiding in her. But the need to talk into a friendly ear was paramount.

'Wait here for a moment,' I said.

I unlocked the shop and went through into the workshop. On the high shelf, I found exactly what I had feared. Holding it by the rim through my handkerchief, I carried it back to the kitchen and laid it on the table. 'This is what's bothering me,' I said.

She looked at it with her head on one side in puzzlement, as well she might. Superficially, it was no more than a piece of steel tube, less than three-quarters of an inch in diameter, with a rim round one end and a small hole up the middle. An unpleasant weapon with which to be knocked on the head, or in my case poked in the stomach, but of no more significance than any old club or pick-handle.

'What is it?' she asked at last. She looked again, carefully. She did not shoot but she had been around guns. 'It looks a bit long to be a blank cartridge adaptor.'

'You're not far off,' I told her. I sat down across the table from her and we both looked at the innocent-seeming tube. 'It's a rifled adaptor tube. Put it in one barrel of a twelve-bore shotgun and you can fire two-two rifle cartridges or blanks out of it. It's remarkably accurate once you get the knack of using it without conventional sights.'

'What on earth do you keep a thing like that for? You have a rifle,' she pointed out.

'It comes in handy sometimes. With this in one barrel of a double-barrel shotgun you can fire blanks, live rifle rounds or shot. I don't use it often, but when the rabbits are thick on the ground and I'm re-training a dog which has got unsteady, I can take the dog out and practise it sitting to shot with blanks, then knock off a distant rabbit for a long retrieve without exposing the dog to temptation. Once I think that the lesson's learned, I can start letting the dog hunt for the shotgun.'

'I see that,' Beth said.

'It was on a shelf in the junk room. But when the Sergeant was here I couldn't see it. So I took a look later and it was gone. Now it's back.'

'You're sure it wasn't there? Not behind something?'

'It was at the front just now. But no, I can't be sure. I was feeling a bit woozy and you know how easy it is to look at something and not see it because you've seen it a thousand times and it's become part of the scenery.'

'You think the murderer was after it?'

I suppressed a sigh. 'Have a bit of sense,' I said. 'The murder had already happened. I think he was trying to put it back. I didn't come back from the hotel by accident. I was meant to hear the dogs and come back hot-foot with the keys. How much have you heard about the murder?'

Beth turned pink, looking younger than ever. 'Only what Mr Kitts told me in the hotel, that that awful Daiches woman had been strangled by her own scarf.'

'I don't know much more than you do,' I said, 'but it seems that she was shot first and then finished off by strangulation.'

'You mean,' she said carefully, 'that the murderer wouldn't be trying to take it when he'd already done his shooting? You think that he used this thing?'

'I'm very much afraid that he may have done.'

Before I could stop her, she put out a hand and picked up the tube. She must have seen my hand jerk because she looked up. 'Is something wrong?'

'You shouldn't have handled it,' I said. 'Fingerprints.'

She reached behind her for a duster and began to polish the outer surface. 'But who'd know that you had a thing like that?'

The damage was already done. I took the tube out of her hands and I looked through the barrel. It had certainly been fired. I gave it back to her. 'Almost anybody who'd been in the shop while the workshop door was open could have seen it on the shelf. Not everyone would have recognised it, but some would. And they could have talked to somebody else. Or, of course, somebody could have seen me shooting the odd rabbit with a shotgun. Most people would know the difference between the boom of a twelve-bore shotgun and the sharp crack of a two-two rifle. It wouldn't take much effort to figure out that I had to have an adaptor. And wasn't the shop left unlocked for most of Thursday?'

'That's right,' she said. 'You thought that I'd locked it and I thought that Mrs Kitts had. Somebody nosy could have looked in your workshop, seen the thing and taken it. We'll have to call the police.'

'Not yet,' I said.

Beth, who had started to get up, subsided gently into her chair. 'Why ever not?' I could almost see her mind struggling with the idea that one might not want to tell everything to the police.

'It's almost a long story. Before you came, I was invited to visit a friend in Spain. I quite fancied a respite in the sunshine. I was due to visit the London School of Tropical Medicine anyway, so Isobel said that if I was going as far as London I might just as well go the rest of the way. She took over and managed, along with Maggie, the kennel-maid we had before you. I went off to stay with my friend in Spain. I took my gun with me and we did a little gentle shooting. I came back feeling a mile better. I'd complied with the formalities and the Customs never even looked at my gun. When I got home, I found that I still had my friend's adaptor tube in one barrel. I'd been knocking off crows which were in the habit of predating on the partridge eggs.

'I phoned him straight away, but he said to keep it. He had several others.

'Well, that was all very well. I made up my mind to get it added to my firearms certificate. But then I realised that, in effect, I had smuggled it into the country. If I applied for a variation to my firearms certificate, the police were going

94

to expect the usual notification from the dealer I bought it from. I could have explained, but I had another bad patch and I just kept putting it off.

'Any time up to now I could probably have found a way round it. But, today, the first thing I knew about any murder was when a police sergeant turned up wanting to take away my rifle. He also seemed to suspect me of boring-out a dummy launcher and shooting the old biddy with that. I was expecting him to spot the adaptor. I was going to say, "Oh yes, I forgot to tell you about that," but he didn't and I dithered and never quite made up my mind to mention it. After he'd gone I went back and looked and it wasn't there any more. It's going to look like hell if I suddenly tell them about it now, especially after you've wiped off any prints from it.'

Beth sometimes looked her prettiest when she frowned but I could have done without being frowned at just then. 'I think you're going to have to,' she said. 'Taken along with somebody half-strangling you with your scarf, this has to be important evidence in a murder.'

'I'm afraid there's more,' I said miserably. 'If I 'fess up now, the police aren't going to be too pleased with me.'

'Serve you right if you get a smacked bottom,' she said, but without smiling.

'It's more serious than that. I've committed an offence under the Firearms Act. Not a very serious offence, but if the police were peevish with me at the time, as they would be, they could prosecute. If they got a conviction, I'd be debarred from keeping even a shotgun. I make my living – and yours and Isobel's – breeding and training dogs. How could I train gundogs and bring them up to field trials standard if I wasn't allowed to keep a gun?'

'Isobel could get a certificate and keep the gun,' she said promptly. 'Or me.'

'And if I laid hands on it I'd be committing another offence. I could be jugged.'

She studied me in silence for a few seconds. 'You aren't

thinking of just getting rid of it and saying nothing?'

There was nothing I would have liked better to do but I still had some conscience left. 'No,' I said. 'If the worst comes to the worst, we may still have to come forward with it. On the other hand, if we were caught trying to throw it in the river or something, how would it look?'

'Terrible,' Beth said.

'Another delay wouldn't make the offence noticeably worse. I think we should sit tight and see what develops. They may catch their murderer tomorrow and be able to prove the strangulation.'

'That might not be a lot of help,' she said. 'They wouldn't forget to ask about the bullet. If the game was up and he was confessing, the first thing he'd say would be, "I borrowed an adaptor out of John Cunningham's junk room".'

She had picked the damnedest time to start being logical. 'He might not. He might say, "You're so bloody clever, you find out." Or we could always call him a liar,' I said.

She pulled a face. 'I don't like it one bit. We can't just pop it into a cupboard and forget it. We could be helping a murderer to get away with killing an old woman. The next person he kills might be somebody . . . '

'Somebody we like?'

She flushed. 'I wasn't going to say that. Well, perhaps I was. But taking the risk of putting it back instead of getting rid of it makes me think that he wants to put the blame on you.' She looked at me, wide-eyed, while we both gave uncomfortable consideration to the thought. 'Whether or not they get a confession or an anonymous letter or something,' she went on, 'they're liable to be round here any day with a search warrant and the metal detectors and things. But if it's really upsetting you – and I can see that it is – I suppose I'd better do something about it.' She looked down at the duster in her hands. 'Leave it to me. Go and have a bath, get into bed and read until you've relaxed. I'll pop you in a hot drink later, if you're still awake.'

There were a thousand things which I should have said and done, but I felt as limp as a wet paper handkerchief and I was happy to leave it all to somebody else, even to Beth. I did as she said.

# NINE

I woke for a little while during the night, confused and shivering, but after that I slept well. I was up in good time on a cold, bright Sunday morning, refreshed, concerned but with no time to worry about it. Isobel, although a tireless partner during the week, usually took Sundays off.

Most Sundays were restful, but to a limited degree. The dogs were given a day to forget the sins and bad habits of the previous week but they still had to be fed, cleaned, brushed and exercised. Over and above which, they had to be paid attention. Half the art of training is to keep the dogs happy even when unoccupied.

The second Sunday of each month, however, was given over to what I called, with inexcusable vanity, my 'Masterclass'. This consisted of a variable number of dog-owners who were prepared to come and, for a fee, be put through their paces along with their dogs. Some came once or twice or until the pupil was firmly on the rails; others appreciated that they were being trained as trainers and persisted for months or years. One man enjoyed it so much that he came regularly from Aberdeen long after he must have known all my precepts by heart and with a dog which was now becoming too old to work let alone to learn anything. It was a social as well as an educational event and I enjoyed it as much as any of them.

That Sunday, there was snow on the high ground and many travellers, including the Aberdonian, had been deterred by the state of the roads. But six turned up. We worked out of doors in the extended garden, ignoring a chilly wind. I started off as usual by putting them through basic exercises, sitting, staying, heeling, coming, sitting at a distance, elementary retrieving and directing by hand signals. As we reached the limit of each dog's ability, I would set the pair some practice exercises and move on. Beth went off with a man whose springer would not sit to command at a distance; she would keep the dog on the lead and make it sit whenever its master, from increasing distances, gave the order.

The last to drop out was a clever young Labrador bitch which had only attended once before. The owner, a stout man in bright green tweeds, was almost seething with frustration. She would, he explained, do almost everything except deliver to hand, preferring to run around with the dummy, just beyond his reach. The classic cure was to run off in the opposite direction, calling for the dog to follow, but 'There's a limit to how long you can go on doing that,' he said. 'I'd look a right Charlie on a big shoot, running off so that the bastard'll follow me with a pheasant.'

That, I had to admit, was true. The bitch would probably not do the same with a real bird – unless the habit was allowed to become engrained. The Labrador, I discovered, only got a dummy in her mouth at the moment of the retrieve. Naturally she was reluctant to give up this splendid toy by which her master set such store. 'Make her carry it at heel, on the lead,' I said. 'When she's so fed up with it that she spits it out, you're probably half-way there. Off you go.'

The first dog to have dropped out – indeed, he could hardly be said to have started – had been Ben. His owners were still trying to induce him to sit, but he was both too strong and too bewildered for them. He was a beautiful, very large, year-old liver and white springer with one of the handsomest heads that I ever saw, long and elegant and patterned with what I could only think of as 'designer' spots. His tail was undocked and, like his legs, beautifully feathered. If I had not known at first glance that he was show-bench and not working bred, the fact that he barely recognised his own name except as a call to food would have confirmed it. He was not my sort of a dog. But he had an affectionate nature and a sort of charm. I could hardly have guessed the passive but crucial part which he was destined to play.

His owners were a young couple. She was noticeably pregnant and close to tears. They had done everything by the book but Ben, although he loved people, could not understand that the noises which humans emitted were intended to convey any message to him. He was a loveable dog and they were reluctant to part with him, but, as the young woman said, he was strong and impetuous and when the baby was born she would never be able to manage a pram with Ben hauling on the lead. It would break their hearts, but if he could not learn to walk reliably to heel and to sit when told, he would have to go – to a good home if possible, but if not . . .

I worked with them for a while. There are ways of tricking a dog into sitting and I thought that we were making progress. But others needed my attention. A lady who hoped to become a picker-up on her husband's shoot had little idea as to how much she should be expecting from her Labrador and I fetched out one of my older dogs and let her get the feel of the handler's job. The man with the other Labrador came back. I took him off to the long cul-de-sac between the house and the barn. It was a place which I had used for the same purpose before. A dog which was doing a retrieve there could only come straight back because there was nowhere else to go. 'Try it,' I said. 'Don't stare at him as he comes back, but give him all the praise in the world if he does it right and then do it again and again.'

Eventually the Masterclass broke up. Several of them had become friends and went off for a lunch at the hotel. Sometimes I would join them, but Ben's owners were waiting behind so I passed up the invitation. I took them into the large, bright sitting room which was little used except for entertainment and for business discussions. They wanted to know my terms for boarding and training a pupil. I gave them a Xeroxed page of breakdown.

The young man, a Mr Sturges, did not seem put off by my prices. Ben must have been held in an esteem which he had done nothing to deserve. Sturges hardly glanced at the page before he nodded. 'If we left him with you for, say, a month, could you do anything with him?'

'I don't usually take dogs which aren't going to do a job of work,' I said. 'I'll stretch a point and take Ben if you like. After all, he is a spaniel of a sort. I think I could do some good. But I can't give any guarantee. It would be up to you and at your risk. I'm sorry, but that's the way it has to be.'

Sturges nodded. 'We understand that,' he said. 'Look, we're not the gambling sort but we like a flutter now and again. If you were a bookie, what odds would you give on being able to turn him into an acceptable house-dog?'

'About evens,' I said. 'Or maybe six to four on.'

They looked at each other, which was all the consultation necessary. 'We'll leave him,' the wife said. 'If you find that he won't learn . . . we wouldn't want to see him again. Perhaps you could give him to somebody, or have him put down. We might buy one of your pups.'

'I could find you something more suitable,' I said tactfully. As I had told the Sergeant, I never sold my pups to non-shooting homes. It would have been like selling a favourite daughter into a harem. A dog is happiest doing what it was bred for, and very few breeds were intended to be pets. 'Has he had all his shots?' I asked.

Sturges produced the inoculation record from a folder. It was up to date.

'If you have his pedigree there, leave it with me,' I said.

Sturges frowned. 'Is that usual?'

'No. But my partner likes it. She runs computer programs on canine genealogy. It's her substitute to knitting or doing the pools. Anyway, I'll need it if I have to try and find a home for him.'

They gave me the pedigree. Beth took Ben for a walk while they made their escape. When he returned to find them gone he seemed puzzled rather than perturbed, as though he had mislaid something but could not remember what or where.

'He's nice,' Beth said, 'but he's as thick as porridge.' Ben, realising that he was the focus of attention, waved his plumed tail.

The Masterclass was for fun and public relations. After a late lunch, we set about the real work of the day.

A trained gundog is not only a valuable commodity. It is also a living being to whom we owe the care which they cannot give themselves. My own illness was a constant reminder about infection. Dogs are as vulnerable to gastro-enteritis as we are and have several diseases of their own. So, at the risk of being called a fusspot (which I never was to my face), I insisted that our level of hygiene should never fall below that which we would expect for ourselves. While Beth fed the puppies and dealt with the kennels and runs, I sterilised the feed dishes and then washed every dummy which had been used, set them to dry in the barn and brought out a fresh set. I seemed to own more dummies than a flourishing maternity hospital.

I was just finishing when the sound of the phone fetched me into the house. Henry's voice came on the other end. 'Isobel's gone off visiting,' he said. 'I'm fed up on my own. Care to come over for a drink? Bring Beth if you like. In fact, bring her anyway. A pretty girl around the house helps to keep my last remaining hormone circulating.'

'I'd rather not leave the place,' I said. 'And I don't want to leave Beth on her own. Not if somebody's buggering about. Come here, if you like. There's gin or whisky and some cans of lager.'

'Coffee would do,' he said. 'I'm half pissed already. But that doesn't matter because Isobel took the car. I'll walk over. I was in the hotel at lunchtime.'

'I guessed that much.'

'Got some more information. I'll be about half an hour.'

I went to tell Beth and found her measuring out feed for the adult dogs' main meal. 'Henry's coming over for coffee in about half an hour,' I said. 'That is, if he can walk it in half an hour with several pints leaking out of him. Can you cope?'

'Yes, of course,' she said. 'I'll bring coffee in as soon as he's here. You go and sit down. In the sitting room,' she added firmly.

'Henry's quite happy in the kitchen.'

'I'm not happy with him in the kitchen. It's the wrong place for guests.'

It was never worth arguing with Beth on that subject. 'Give Ben his dinner now and I'll take him with me.' This was our first peaceful moment alone together. 'What did you do with the you-know-what?' I asked her.

'I don't think I should tell you. Then if somebody asks about it, you can say that you don't know where there'd be a thing like that around here.' If a woman can tell the truth in a way that totally obscures its meaning, she feels that she has not sinned.

Ben wolfed his meal. I took him outside for a few minutes to relieve himself.

The sitting room, which some previous owner had thrown together with a former dining room, was large and pleasantly old-fashioned, being furnished with some relics from the family home which my mother had once re-covered with what I suppose was chintz. The pastel colours looked well against the pale walls. The carpet was good but too old for dog-hairs to matter. Beth had hung a few pictures and filled a large vase with a fan of

103

twigs bearing copper beech leaves. The room was warm but the space, the colours and the comparative bareness made it look cold. I put a match to the fire. The logs from our fallen oak began to spread a cheerful glow.

Ben was relieved at having been fed but he still felt lost in his new surroundings. I wanted to get the measure of him, but first I had to get and keep his attention despite such interesting competition as a leaf fluttering against the window, dancing firelight or a noise in the chimney. Pandering to gluttony is not often a good basis for training, but there are times when it is easier to fix the dog's attention by the reward of tidbits and to break the habit of expectation later. Ben was, I had found, almost indifferent to the small chocolate-flavoured sweets which I usually use for the purpose but he turned out to be addicted to salted peanuts. He realised at last that the only way to get the peanuts was by giving me his undivided attention. We began to make a little progress. When Henry arrived, not long behind his promised time, Ben was sitting on command twice out of three times.

Henry recognised Ben immediately for what he was. 'A beautiful nincompoop,' he said as he eased himself down into a chair. 'You surely don't think you're going to make anything of him?'

'He'll never make a shooter's dog,' I admitted. 'If I can turn him into a biddable pet, his owners will be satisfied.'

'If you can, they'll probably do a sacrifice to you. Preferably of that dim beast,' Henry added as Ben tried to lick his face.

Beth brought the coffee in and poured it. 'The dogs have been fed,' she said. 'Samson didn't seem to fancy his dinner much. I think he's a little off-colour. He has a slight temperature and his nose is dry. Perhaps he picked up something yesterday. I've moved him into the isolation kennel.'

'I'll ask Isobel to take a look at him,' I said. 'He's

probably been at the dustbins again. What he's picked up has been some leftover too far gone even for his cast-iron gut.'

'He hasn't been on the loose,' Beth said indignantly. 'And we don't have dustbins any more. What's more, the whole bin-bag's gone. Vanished.'

'Your Sergeant will have taken it,' Henry said. 'They've been collecting refuse bags. Somebody was saying that they get at more truth that way than by taking statements.'

'And no more unsavoury,' I said. 'To the police, the truth usually stinks.'

Beth gave Henry a biscuit and forced a large slice of cake on me. She never missed an opportunity to try to put some weight on my bones. The coffee had, as usual, been percolated from freshly ground beans. With Beth, coffee-making was a ritual. I suspected that she bought only beans which had been picked at a certain phase of the moon and then muttered incantations as it brewed. After so much effort, it always surprised me by tasting slightly less palatable than instant coffee.

The taste reminded me. 'That Sergeant said something about a dog being poisoned,' I said to Henry. 'I think that he said it was one of Mrs Daiches'.'

'If he did, he was leading you up the garden path again,' Henry said. 'Mrs Cory lost one of her bitches late last week. She's down to one now. Somebody threw some meat over the wire, loaded with poison. He probably meant to get both of them, but the older bitch guzzled the lot. The Corys reported it to the police at the time, but otherwise they've kept very quiet about it. Now that the fact's out, of course, she's started going around playing the martyr and accusing absolutely anybody.'

Beth was looking shocked. 'You said something about that last night but I didn't take it in,' she said. 'That's a terrible thing to do! Poisoning a dog, I mean.'

'It is,' I said. 'But it happens.'

'Who'd do such a thing?'

'Sometimes a prospective burglar,' Henry said. 'More often, it turns out to be a neighbour who's fed up at the barking or turds on the pavement or just plain hates the dog's owner. But Olive Cory keeps her dogs in or walks them in the fields. I hadn't heard of any complaints about barking, but I don't suppose anybody would grumble to me.' Henry and Isobel lived in a pair of joined and converted cottages more than a mile beyond the village.

'They barked all right,' I said. 'If you took the path behind her garden without a dog, they barked their stupid heads off. If you had a dog, they only growled. If you think about it, that shows a sort of twisted, Irish logic. But who lives next door to her?'

'Old Tommy Frost,' Beth said.

'Does he indeed?' I said. 'Well, Tommy's as deaf as the proverbial post. So he wouldn't object to barking. And if a relatively quiet shot was fired towards the Daiches' house from the field beyond the fence, only the Corys would be likely to hear it.'

Henry stretched his legs out towards the fireplace. The room was warm from the central heating but the glow of the fire was magnetic. 'We're back to the murder, are we? There's Laurie Duffus, next to the Daiches,' he said. 'But the word is that from the time he came home from work he was out in his back garden with a lamp hanging up, building yet another shed. He can't have much garden left by now. His neighbours say that the noise of hammering never stopped.'

'That's the sort of daft remark people make,' I said, 'because they're only aware of the noise while it's happening. Nobody could hammer all the time. They have to stop to fetch more boards or cut them. The hammering could have stopped for ten minutes and they wouldn't have noticed.'

'And there's Mr Daiches himself,' Beth said. 'He'd surely have heard a shot if he was at home.'

'He wasn't,' Henry said. 'That's why she wasn't found

until morning. He went down to Edinburgh for a weekend course on arbitration. The police had to fetch him back. He probably had more motive than most to put a slug into his wife – they used to fight like terriers – but he's the one person who couldn't have done it.'

'Is a slug the same as a bullet?' Beth asked.

Henry seemed surprised. 'Did I say slug? Sometimes they can be much the same thing. Bullet usually implies something fired by a propellant and a slug comes out of an airgun. It's shaped . . . well, more like yourself, my dear, with a small waist and a skirt. The air pressure expands the skirt to grip the rifling. Perhaps it was a Freudian slip. You see, Ian West – the redhaired man who keeps the shop, you know him? – he seems to have got himself into trouble with the law. Mr Cory had to account for his own movements, just like anybody else, and he was flighting pigeon with Ian keeping him company until about four. Not that that would do either of them much good. I hear that the pathologist fixed the time of death at around six in the evening, at which time it was her custom to go out and feed her dogs.'

'Had they been fed?' I asked.

'So I'm told,' Henry said. 'Her murderer must have caught her on her way back to the house. Which gives me a convenient alibi. I was in the hotel and talking to Neill Cory and some others from opening time onward.' Henry sounded rather disappointed at being struck off the list of suspects.

'How on earth do you find out that sort of thing?' I asked. Henry's snippets were usually very reliable whereas local news seemed to pass me by. Once, I had enquired after the health of somebody who had already died.

'They found something en route towards her tummy,' Henry said with an apologetic glance at Beth. 'In tracing her last movements, they were asking around for anybody who shared tea and biscuits with her. One of the constables was a little more forthcoming than the others, that's all.'

'You're getting away from the other point,' Beth complained. 'What's Ian West done?'

'Oh yes,' Henry said. 'Sorry! Your revered employer asked a couple of irrelevant questions. It seems that Ian had a powerful two-two airgun that he brought back from Germany after the war. He used it for knocking off rats around the back of the shop. When the police called on him at home to ask about the times during which Neill Cory was filling the air with the sound of gunfire, there it was standing behind his front door where anybody could have borrowed it. He'd never got a certificate for it.'

'But I still don't understand. You don't need a certificate for an airgun,' Beth said. 'Or do you?'

'You do if it has more than a certain maximum pressure,' Henry told her kindly. 'Fifteen foot-pounds, I seem to recall. Ian's bad luck was that the policeman who came to his door was an airgun enthusiast. This was one of the pump-up ones with a reservoir. If you pumped it up all the way, it would be about as powerful as a rifle.'

'More powerful,' I said. 'I've seen one of those put a slug clean through a telegraph pole. And it was still quieter than a small-bore rifle.'

'If you have to pump it up,' Beth said, 'I suppose it would be slower to reload?'

'Much slower,' Henry said. 'Of course, Ian West hadn't much use for either of the ladies, but if he was going to knock off the females of the species he'd have started with Olive Cory. She sold him a pup once, in both senses of the term.'

I hardly heard what they were saying. If Ian West's air-weapon was suspect, I might be off the hook. On the other hand, friends might be falling into trouble because I was too timid to face up to facts.

Henry might advise me. He was a wily old chap and quite capable of holding his tongue. I was on the point of speaking when we recognised the sound of Henry's car driving up to the house. The dogs must also have recognised it, because although the microphones were alive we heard only one short bark from the kennels. Ben, dozing at my feet, raised his head as if hoping that his owners might have returned for him and lowered it again with a sigh.

Isobel came in and ungraciously accepted coffee. She was peevish but not noticeably hungover. She asked how I was feeling after the previous night's excitement.

'I went to see my niece,' she said, without giving me time to reply. 'She has a new boyfriend and didn't want to know. Henry wasn't at home and he wasn't in the pub and this is the only other place he ever goes. Anyway, I wanted to do a little homework from my records. What on earth is that object doing here?' she added suddenly, glaring at Ben. 'It looks like one of those useless animals they breed down in the village.'

'His owners came to the Masterclass,' I explained. 'They want me to have him put down if I can't drum some basic obedience into him.'

'I don't give much for his chances. One thing about dogs, they don't know when they're doomed,' Isobel said, scratching Ben absently behind the ear. 'They have no concept of death at all. I'll be surprised if you can teach that creature to walk without its back legs tripping up the front ones. Anyway, Joe Little wants me to recommend a stud-dog for Aholibah. There's a touch of hip dysplasia well back in her pedigree so he wants a stud-dog who's clear, 'way back to the first wolf. I'm exaggerating,' she explained kindly to Beth, who was looking puzzled. 'But not very much.'

That reminded me. I fetched the notes which I had taken over the phone. 'Mr Hordle of the Eye Panel was on the phone,' I said.

Isobel scanned the notes rapidly and nodded. 'This fills in a gap,' she said.

Isobel had kept up her connection with the RCVS

and from that and other sources she maintained, in the kennel office, remarkably comprehensive records of congenital faults in all gundog breeds, including even the show strains. Her vast accumulation of paper was a nuisance at times in the tiny and overstressed office; at other times, it was a godsend. Our ability to warrant a pup free from congenital defects brought us a steady trickle of paying customers. Gradually, Isobel was transferring the data to computer discs, consolidating a pool of information often consulted by other breeders.

'While you're at it,' I said, 'we'll be needing a stud for Burgundy before much longer. Samson could do the job, but they're cousins.'

Isobel groaned and looked put-upon, but I knew that she considered her researches to be near the hub of the canine universe, second in importance only to the results of field trials. She would have been lost without her hobby. 'And the part of the pedigree that they share isn't the best part,' she said. 'I know. I'll get onto it in plenty of time.'

'I'm sure,' I told her. 'But remember that Burgundy's seasons come round in less than six months.'

She snorted. 'And you remember that we decided to run her in a Novice Trial next weekend. You've more need to be giving her a final polish than trying to teach me to suck eggs.' Either Henry had proved to be a disappointment or she was still feeling the effects of the previous day's indulgence.

'Sorry, grandma,' I said.

She smiled reluctantly. 'I'm not even old enough to be your mother,' she said, 'so don't come it. You three go and leave me in peace. Go down to the hotel and have the drink you didn't have time to finish last night.'

'You go,' Beth said. 'I'll stay.'

Isobel gave a ladylike shudder. 'I don't really feel much like a drink today,' she said, 'for some reason. And I'd like to get some work done. I'll bring the papers in here, where there's a fire and plenty of table space. Leave the loudspeaker on and I'll keep an ear open for the dogs.'

'Hark a bark and buzz the fuzz,' Henry said. It was one of his favourite little jokes.

'Just go.'

When Isobel was in an autocratic mood there was nothing to do but obey. We rose – Henry hopefully, Beth obediently and myself with resignation. 'You might look in on Samson,' I said. 'He's in the isolation kennel. Beth says that he's off-colour. Refused his meal tonight.'

Isobel finished putting up the leaves of the gate-leg table before replying. 'I'll look at him,' she said. 'If that greedy bastard isn't eating, something's up. Gastro-enteritis, probably. Now, for God's sake, go.'

While Henry emptied his delicate bladder, Beth and I paid a call on Samson in the isolation kennel. Samson was looking rather sorry for himself and swallowing at irregular intervals. He had sicked tidily in a corner of the run and Beth insisted on cleaning up the mess and returning to the house for a wash before we set off.

I took Ben with me on a leather slip-lead. It was a good opportunity to start training him to heel. Almost as an afterthought, I fetched Scoter to accompany us. She was a motherly little soul and, if they got to know each other, I could kennel them together with a fair chance of a night's sleep undisturbed by howling from an unhappy newcomer. A newcomer would usually be banished to the isolation kennel, but Samson was already in occupation. Anyway, Ben's owners had gone overboard with inoculations. And he seemed remarkably free of parasites. Either that, or he was too stupid to scratch.

# TEN

Ben was determined to forge ahead, but when he found that he achieved nothing but to choke himself in the slip-lead he steadied down. A few good jerks on the lead reminded him how to walk at heel. Gentleness is usually a virtue in training, but Ben's owners, I decided, had tried to handle him too softly.

We took the path through the fields. It was dark and the moon was only a faint promise in the eastern sky, but Beth led the way with a torch. As we passed behind the Corys' house, a dog growled from the kennel at the bottom of the garden.

'If she lost another dog last week,' I said, 'she'll be down to the one young bitch she kept from the last litter. Too young to breed from just yet. Or has she been shopping for replacements?'

'She's been asking around,' Beth said, 'but I haven't heard that she found anything suitable yet. She seems to want championship stock at a "good home" price. And you've got to be careful with show spaniels if you want to breed. Other breeders tend not to part with the good ones.'

'That's for sure,' I said. I always tried to keep the best for myself.

'Olive wasn't always so fussy,' Henry said out of the darkness.

'She'll hear you,' Beth whispered.

But we could have stood in Mrs Cory's front garden,

slandering her at the tops of our voices, without her hearing a word of it. Before we had even entered the hotel I could hear her unmistakable voice, both shrill and penetrating, raised in furious argument.

'We could go somewhere else,' Beth said.

'There isn't anywhere else,' I pointed out. 'And if there were, I wouldn't let that harpy drive me away.'

As we entered, Mrs Cory finished a tirade which seemed to be directed mainly at Laurie Duffus. She turned away and found herself face to face with me. Her pointed face was pink with temper. 'And as for you . . . ' she began.

General conversation, which had resumed, broke off again. Her husband, Neill, tried to fade away. His back suggested that he had never seen the woman before. Henry and Beth vanished into a corner.

'What about me?' I asked gently. I guessed that she was only looking for a victim.

Perhaps I looked amused – something in my face seemed to infuriate her. 'You think you're bloody clever, but you're not. Poor Laura was right. You breed hideous, cruel dogs.'

'But clever,' I said. With the late Mrs Daiches, who had on occasions been capable of almost reasonable discussion, I would have pointed out that, so far from being cruel, one of the prime purposes of a gundog was the quick recovery of wounded game for immediate despatch. But Mrs Cory had never been ready for a two-sided debate.

She snorted and changed the subject. 'I've seen you shooting from an upstairs window,' she said. 'And I could see that window from the place where Laura was killed.'

'That would be an incredible shot at the distance and in the dark,' I said.

'You'd have had . . . I didn't mean from there and you know it!' She was winding herself up into fury but there were real tears in her eyes. 'None of you really gives a damn that Laura's gone. You hated her and she hated the lot of you and now you're laughing up your sleeves.

Nobody cares except me. You're . . . unfeeling, the lot of you,' she told the company in general. Then she switched back to me. 'I know what I know. And that girl's making a fool out of you. Get out of my way.'

She pushed past, thumping me with the heavy handbag which was always over her arm, and stumped out of the hotel. Her husband emerged from a hiding place behind a pair of large farmers. 'John, I'm sorry about that,' he said. 'Let me buy you a drink.'

'I'm with the others,' I said. 'I'll buy them. How do you put up with her? Or is she different in the house?'

'Just the same,' he said. He managed a smile. 'Consistency is a great virtue in a woman.' He was a short man, rotund and balding, with an air combining amusement with determination. I supposed that he needed both. On most weekdays he commuted to St Andrews where he had an office dealing in property.

At the bar, I found myself standing alongside Laurie Duffus. He was soberer than he had been the night before and nodded a non-committal greeting. He had a full glass, to my relief. I felt disinclined to buy him a drink after his insults of the previous evening. I caught the eye of Flora the barmaid – an opulent young lady with bright hair and a toothy smile. I bought poor Neill a whisky – he was always thought of and referred to as 'poor Neill' – and took drinks to Henry and Beth who had settled at a table.

Back at the bar for my Guinness, I asked Neill, 'What the hell was she getting at?'

'Damned if I know,' he said. 'She gets bees in her bonnet sometimes.'

'Was she insinuating something about Beth and me?'

'Forget it, John. She was just havering.'

'No,' I said. 'I want to know.'

He hesitated and then shrugged. 'She thinks Beth's after you for your money.'

The idea was so silly that I laughed in his face. 'You can tell her from me,' I said, 'that I don't have any and that Beth wouldn't be after it if I did. She works for me, full stop.'

'I'll tell her. But she won't believe it. She aye believes the worst of others – which I suppose is only fair,' he added. 'Folk are always ready to believe the worst of her. She has a heart, you know.'

I nodded. Something had to keep the acidulated blood circulating in her crabby veins. But the expression had another meaning. 'You don't mean heart trouble?'

'Nothing like that,' he said earnestly. 'I mean that she cares. She's feeling Laura's death deeply. Put it down to that and forget it. Please, John.'

Some crony invited Neill for a game of pool in the back room. He made a half-hearted attempt to return my drink but I let him escape. From what I had heard, his business had suffered with the slump in property values and he was saddled with the expenses of his wife's imminent lawsuit.

Scoter had taken her favourite place before the fire, displacing by force of personality an elderly couple who had been warming their joints. Ben was leaning against my leg, holding onto his only sheet-anchor in a strange world.

'She must be bloody good in bed,' Laurie said suddenly, turning round on the stool beside me.

'Who must?' I thought that he was referring to Beth, or possibly to Isobel, and I was quite ready to resume our quarrel of the previous evening.

'Neill's wife.'

'You think so?' I was puzzled. Mrs Cory had a face like a spadeful of raisins and the rest of her could have been mistaken for a sack of dogfood. The intolerance which she showed to local lovers suggested that she had never regarded sex as anything but an aberration.

'Why else would he have put up with her for all these years?'

It was a tenable theory, but I had been told that Neill's business had been wholly financed by his wife's money. As a marriage, in fact, it was more of a business partnership. But it seemed a pity to disabuse Laurie of illusions which were certain some day to rebound to Mrs Cory's discredit, causing that disseminator of malicious and unfounded gossip extreme annoyance and embarrassment.

'As a matter of fact . . . ' I said.

'Aye?'

I assured him, on good authority but in confidence, that she was notoriously expert in certain sexual practices which are not usually referred to in polite conversation, and hoped to God that he would never mention me as the originator of the rumours which were bound to follow.

Laurie nodded, seeming pleased to have his supposition confirmed, and no doubt filed the information away for future use as ammunition. 'You only got the backlash of her tongue,' he said. 'It started when she got the wrong change. Then she turned on me. The old bitch tried to suggest that I'd killed her bosom buddy, although I'd been out in my garden the whole time. The neighbours were complaining about the noise I made.'

'Did you hear a shot?' I asked idly.

'No. But I wouldn't. I was hammering. And you know how echoes come back from other houses. I did hear her voice, once, though I didn't hear what she said. Likely she was only speaking to her dogs. I told the police, and if they're satisfied I don't see why she has to stir it up.'

'She's a born stirrer-up.' I could have added that in my opinion Mrs Cory's only useful function in the world was as a topic of conversation.

'You're not wrong. I'll tell you something else I told the police. About a week ago, I heard Ma Daiches' voice. I don't know who she was speaking to, she was round the corner from me, but it surely wasn't the dogs. She said "Just don't come near me again until this is settled".'

He seemed to be expecting some reaction so I said 'Golly!' in a respectful tone. 'Why does Mrs Cory have her knife into you?' I asked.

'When did she ever need anything to go on about? I gave her a slanging a fortnight ago for taking a kick at one of my dogs and she'd been waiting for a chance to get even. This time, she started narking at me for keeping ferrets, said that the smell upset her dogs and that they were vicious little brutes and rabbits never did anybody any harm. And me a market gardener! I'd be eaten out of my livelihood by rabbits if I let them be. Her trouble is, she doesn't think any neighbour this side of Balmoral would be good enough to live next door to her or her bloody friends.'

'She wouldn't get on with the neighbours, living next door to Balmoral Castle, if she's in the habit of kicking Labradors,' I said.

Laurie laughed and looked as though he might be on the point of offering to buy me a drink. 'The stupid old cow had taken one of her bitches out in high season,' he said. 'Thought that a good spray around the hindquarters with air freshener was adequate birth control, for God's sake! At least Mrs Daiches kept her buggers under control. When Nova wandered over for a good sniff and a climb aboard, she gave him a boot in the ribs.'

I would probably have done the same, but there seemed to be no percentage in saying so. 'Personally,' I said, 'I'm sick and tired of asking people not to be nice to my dogs. How can you keep a dog's full attention when it thinks that any human figure is a heaven-sent source of petting and tidbits?'

He grinned maliciously. 'I don't know,' he said. 'But you're going to have to try.' I followed his eyes. The elderly couple were feeding Scoter potato crisps. 'You still want to back your dogs against mine at retrieving, for a hundred quid?'

'Any time. Make it a thousand if you like,' I said. 'I'll choose the time and place. Either of your present dogs, with you handling. I'll choose one of mine and you can decide whether I handle it, or Mrs Kitts or Beth. Straightforward

117

retrieving of dummies from cover, marked and unmarked. Joe Little can judge.'

I left him and went to collect Scoter. When he thought over my terms I knew that he would not take me up on the bet. I could pick a place thick with rabbits and a time after the population had recovered from winter and the recent myxomatosis outbreak. Either of his present dogs could be counted on to give chase and be disqualified. It takes a clever trainer to shoot rabbits over a Labrador without teaching the dog to run in.

The bar was full but the crowd was thinner than it had been on the previous evening. Either we were earlier or the novelty of a murder in our midst was already wearing off. Henry and Beth had managed to find seats at a small table in a corner. I borrowed a spare stool from another table and joined them, settling the two spaniels in the corner where they curled up companionably together.

'Facts are continuing to emerge,' Henry said, 'and very interesting they are too. It seems that one of our local constables has for some time been smitten with our Flora and that she is now smiling on him in exchange for fragments of information to satisfy her curiosity and that of her customers. I gather that the rate of exchange is one smile per fragment, so one can only speculate as to what she may have given away in exchange for the volume of information now circulating. Unfortunately, he is not very close to the heart of the matter. Nor am I very close to the heart of Flora, although when I was half my present age I would have made every effort to get closer.'

'I bet you were a devil,' Beth said.

'I was. But that,' Henry said carefully, 'was before I married. It is also beside the point, which is that what we are hearing is several places removed from the horse's mouth.'

Now that he came to mention a horse's mouth, it occurred to me that Flora's toothy smile did sometimes look rather equine. 'And what are we hearing?' I asked.

'That we had not been misled,' Henry said. 'There was no bullet in the body.' For a moment, I felt an upsurge of hope. Henry quashed it immediately. 'It had passed clean through,' he said. 'The pathologist detected traces of lead where it had glanced off a rib. When I walked over to visit you, I noticed a line of fed-up-looking bobbies scouring the stubble behind the Daiches' house and had a guess at what they were looking for. The search continues, so far without success.'

I avoided Beth's eye. I was far from sure whether this was good news or bad. The discovery of the bullet would enable the weapon to be identified . . . if the weapon fell into the hands of the police. 'Anything else?' I asked, to turn the subject.

'Plenty, but none that makes any sense, considered in a vacuum. The superintendent in charge is playing his cards close to the chest, as they say. Junior officers are being sent to ask people the most extraordinary questions without any explanation being given them as to why it should be wanted. Flora's boyfriend, for example, was sent to find out whether the late Mrs Daiches had been addicted to Coca-Cola.'

'The pathologist probably detected it in her stomach,' I said.

'Very possible,' Henry said doubtfully. 'Although tea and biscuits are all that has been mentioned to date. I really can't visualise anyone as fastidious as Laura Daiches mixing Coca-Cola with her afternoon tea. But why couldn't they just ask her husband? Unless, of course, he's under suspicion despite what would seem on cursory examination to be a bomb-proof alibi. Husbands, I believe, very often are suspected. And then the young man was sent to find out whether Laurie Duffus owns a tape-recorder.'

'And does he?' I asked.

'As it turns out, yes. But can you tell me why the police should want to know that?'

'As it happens,' I said, 'I can. Obviously, the police want to know whether Laurie really was hammering in his garden non-stop or whether he could have taped some of his own noise and left it playing back while he lay in wait for Mrs Daiches.'

'But that's silly,' Beth said.

'It might not be,' I said. 'What with dogs and ferrets and the overflow from the market garden, the back garden at Laurie's house is getting so full of sheds that no neighbour could have seen whether he was there or not. He's lived there alone since his wife died. And Mrs Daiches and Laurie were always slanging each other.'

'And both thoroughly enjoying it,' Beth pointed out.

Henry was making noises suggestive of another round. I only hoped that my appetite and capacity for beer would endure until I was his age. He was forestalled by the arrival on our table of a tray of drinks, deposited by Joe Little.

Joe was a heavily built man of above average height, but he was light on his feet despite his great bulk. He was, as usual, better dressed than was common among the dog fraternity. Dog-hairs and muddy paws do not go well with smart suits.

He fetched another stool and joined us. His square face betrayed a slight anxiety. Omitting his usual courtesies, he came straight to the point. 'I want to ask you something,' he said to me.

'Now's your chance,' I said.

'Right.' He looked from Henry to Beth. 'You two may as well listen to this. John, you remember giving me some two-two cartridges the other day?'

'Wednesday,' I said. 'You came to me for blanks for the dummy launcher. I didn't have any. I gave you a dozen live rounds instead.'

He was nodding like one of those dogs in the rear windows of cars. 'I wanted to give two of my dogs some practice in retrieving from water,' he said. 'I was going to St Andrews anyway, so I pulled into the little car park at

120

the Eden Reserve, ready to walk out on Coble Shore. I pulled the bullets, using pliers that I keep in the car, and crimped the ends of the cartridges. They did throw the dummy, as you said they would – not as far as the proper blanks would have done, but far enough for water work. I used them all up. Then I went on into St Andrews.'

'And found a source of the proper Turner Richards blank cartridges and brought back a supply for both of us,' I said helpfully. 'Did the dogs perform all right?'

'Perfectly. Thank God you remember,' he said. He glanced around the bar. Nobody was listening to us but he lowered his voice anyway. 'I was afraid that you might do what they call a willing forget. If the police ask you, will you confirm my story?'

'I'd rather not have to,' I said. Joe's eyebrows went up. 'I won't leave you in the shit,' I said, 'but I'm not supposed to hand on live ammunition to somebody who doesn't have a firearms certificate. It's a piece of bureaucratic rubbish but it happens to be the law. Have you already told the police about it?'

He nodded again. 'I had to,' he said. 'They found some of the bullets in my car and wanted to know where they'd come from.'

'But have you signed a statement?' Beth asked quickly.

'Not yet.'

'When the time comes, couldn't you say that Mr Cunningham pulled the bullets out for you and gave them to you separately? Then he wouldn't have given you live ammunition, would he?'

Joe looked at her in surprise for several seconds. 'I suppose that's right. You're a clever little madam, aren't you?' he said. Like the rest of us, he often fell into the trap of speaking to Beth as though she were still in a gym-slip. 'I could try it on. Don't see that it makes much difference to the police. Not as far as the murder's concerned.'

'It might do,' Henry said suddenly. 'Did they find all the bullets in your car?'

'About half of them,' Joe said. 'I can't think where the rest went.'

'I can think where one of them might have gone,' I said. 'So can Henry. And so can the police. I take it that you were in your jeep, not the estate car?' Joe's jeep, which he had been using on the day he borrowed the cartridges, was a soft-top. A thief would only have had to undo one or two studs in order to reach a door-lock.

'That's right.'

'And the bullets were in full view?'

'In the ash-tray,' he said. 'I don't remember closing it.'

'You're thinking of Ian West's pump-up airgun?' Henry asked.

'Obviously,' I said. 'Like yourself.'

Joe sighed. 'The police asked me all about the jeep's movements. It was parked outside Ian's shop for most of Thursday,' he said. 'The fields around my place are in winter barley just now so I came down to The Moss to give the dogs some training.' He sighed again, finished his pint and got to his feet. 'I knew you wouldn't let me down.' He slapped me on the shoulder and left us.

I ought to have been sad that evidence should be piling up against the inoffensive Ian, but my only emotion was relief that suspicion might be turning away from my adaptor.

'All very complicated,' Henry said. He laughed suddenly. 'Which do you like less, Olive Cory or Andrew Williamson?' he asked me.

'I think it's a dead heat,' I said.

'Well, think about it.' Something seemed to be causing Henry some deep amusement. 'I rarely see either of them these days so I'll pass on another fragment of gossip and leave you to make up your own mind. Laura Daiches promised to give Olive a signed statement about the shooting of the dog, but she died without doing it. I was talking to Neill Cory in here on Friday evening. The subject of the lawsuit came up – as it usually does – and I asked him how confident he was about Laura's evidence. He said that they hadn't got a statement from her yet and he was getting worried.'

'And away goes any motive that the Corys might have had,' I said.

'Not necessarily,' Beth said. 'It would depend which side Mrs Daiches was really on.'

I looked at her in puzzlement. We knew where Mrs Daiches' loyalty had lain.

'I don't mind being ignored while I'm talking rubbish,' Henry grumbled, 'but when I'm telling you something interesting the least you could do is to listen. Olive was in here at lunchtime today, looking for somebody to quarrel with. She tried to pick on me, so, just to be annoying, I asked her whether she'd ever got Laura's statement.'

'And she said that she had?' I suggested. I would have loved to envisage Mrs Cory as a forger.

'No, of course she didn't,' Henry snapped. 'But she did try to shut me up and she got the hell out as quickly as she could. My guess is that she's trying to bluff a settlement out of Andrew's insurers before they find out. So if you happen to prefer Andrew to Olive Cory, go ahead and drop him a hint.'

# ELEVEN

Walking back, Ben seemed to have accepted the discipline of walking at heel. Although it was Sunday evening, the police caravan tucked against the Daiches' fence was bright and busy. A breeze had risen, sharp enough to numb the ears, and I was glad to near the house.

As we reached the front door of the house it opened suddenly and Isobel appeared. When she saw us she jumped and put a hand to her heart. 'Oh, God!' she said.

'What's up?' I asked her. 'Visitors?'

'Nothing's up,' she said, laughing. 'You made me jump, no more than that. No visitors, one phone call and that was a wrong number. And that's been the sum total of interruptions. I've had peace and quiet for once. I visited Samson earlier and I'm just going to take another look at him. It's a gastro-enteritis right enough. Probably not infectious but I've given him an antibiotic injection just in case. A day's starvation and then light diet and he'll be as fit as a flea by the time the Championship comes round.'

'That's a relief,' Henry said. He took as much interest in our successes and failures as any of us. 'We'll come with you and look at the patient. Perhaps I should have brought a bag of grapes.'

'The gluttonous little beggar would be just as pleased with a bag of rotting cabbage leaves,' Isobel said. She had always disapproved of what I looked on as Samson's healthy appetite.

I left them near the isolation kennel. I was just shutting

Ben in with Scoter when voices broke out. They sounded perturbed. I hurried back. The light was on over the isolation kennel's pen. I met Isobel at the gate. She had Samson's limp form in her arms. Beth and Henry were fussing around her.

'Oh God!' I said. 'What's happened now?'

'Look around for yourself,' Isobel said. 'We've had a visit from the poisoner.' She strode off towards the house.

I looked. There were several puddles of sickness but I could see nothing else of significance until a dark plonk near a corner caught my eye. It was a lump of steak. I picked it up. Only a corner had been nibbled. It seemed to have been slit to form a pocket which had been filled with something resembling a popular brand of slug pellets.

I ran after them into the house. Out of habit, as I went through the hall, I would have checked the loudspeaker switch, but I heard Ben whining to himself as I passed one of the speakers.

In a small room which had probably once been a pantry, Isobel had established a simple surgery which met most of our needs. Samson was already on the table, limp and yet twitching. He was making a high whine which set the hairs crawling on my neck. Isobel was making ready the stomach pump.

'Out, the lot of you!' she said. 'I can't be doing with folk looking over my shoulder while I'm working.'

'I think it was slug pellets,' I told her.

'That's what I'm gambling on. Out!'

Beth was already putting the kettle on – her own instinctive response to any crisis. I joined Henry at the dining table.

'Who'd want to hurt Samson?' I asked the world. The shock was hitting me and Samson was no longer one of the fixed points in the universe but a clever and biddable little dog with good manners, always anxious to please. He had contributed as much to our successes from his store of talent as had Isobel or I. Apart from his value at stud, he was the living and working apex of the blood-line which we were struggling to establish. And suddenly he might not be there any longer.

'The same nutter who poisoned one of Mrs Cory's dogs,' Henry said.

'Probably,' Beth said.

'Definitely,' said Henry. 'Slug pellets were used to poison Mrs Cory's bitch. Nobody was after Samson in particular. Score so far, one show bitch and one working stud-dog.'

'This time, are you going to call the police?' Beth asked me.

'This time, yes.' Excitement and worry had brought on the deadly tiredness but I dragged myself out of the chair and through the house. The telephone was inconveniently placed in the small office and we had not yet got around to having extensions installed. There were always more urgent uses for our time and money. Directory Enquiries gave me a number for the caravan which was serving as a temporary Incident Room. Despite the late hour of a Sunday, Sergeant Flodden came on the line and I gave him a brief report.

'He's coming straight up,' I told Henry and Beth. 'He sounded excited.'

'As well he might,' said Henry. 'It's as easy to believe in a single weirdo going around and knocking off – or trying to knock off,' he amended hastily, ' – dogs and people as in a murderer and a separate canicide, if there is such a word, operating in the same area at the same time. Coincidences do happen, but they make a poor basis for theorising about crime.'

The police must have been of the same view because a car arrived within the next minute or two, bringing not only the Sergeant but his Inspector and a brace of constables. While his subordinates went to visit the scene, the Inspector settled down with us in the kitchen. He was a lean man, bald before his time, with a voice which I somehow found irritating.

'A valuable dog, is it?' the Inspector asked.

'Very,' I said. 'Already, he commanded a higher stud fee than you or I will ever do.' (The Inspector gave me a look as if warning me to speak for myself.) 'And if I could have made him up to Champion next month . . . '

'Don't start speaking of him in the past tense,' Henry told me. 'He's still ticking or Isobel would have come out. In case you don't know it, my wife's a vet,' he told the Inspector. 'She's doing the necessary just now.'

'Would he be the most valuable dog in the place?'

'That's hard to tell,' I said. 'None of our breeding stock is for sale.'

'But he was the nearest to the house,' Beth put in.

Her comment was ignored. We were stumbling through a joint explanation of events when Isobel came into the kitchen and our words dried up. I tried to read her face.

'He'll make it,' she said. Three of us started to breathe again. 'He's sleeping now. Three things saved him. Paradoxically, if he hadn't had enteritis he'd have wolfed the lot and he wouldn't have stood a chance. As it was, he just wasn't hungry. Also, I'd visited him only twenty minutes before and there was no meat in his pen. We must have found him soon after he took what little he did manage to swallow. And, finally, we must have guessed right. Slug pellets can be lethal to dogs if you don't act in time.'

Beth put down mugs of a hot drink in front of us. The Inspector took a mug and looked more human. I sipped mine without even noticing what it was.

Isobel began to outline the few events of the evening. The Inspector leaned forward and interrupted her. 'Slug pellets, you said?'

'It seems so. Your analyst can make sure.'

'If so, it's a link with the first poisoning,' the Inspector said.

'It's an insane link,' I said. 'Apart from the fact that they were both dogs, I can't think of anything they had in common. Some nut-case must be responsible.'

'That could be,' the Inspector said dismissively. Questions of sanity were not for him to decide. He had another question ready but was interrupted by the sound of his men's voices over the loudspeakers, followed by uproar from the dogs. 'What on earth's that?' he asked.

I explained about our simple alarm system. He seemed amused. 'That was cheaper than electronic alarms?' he suggested.

'Electronic alarms, used out of doors, go off for birds and animals,' I explained. 'I didn't fancy being fetched out of bed every time an owl flitted by on the hunt for a fieldmouse. Dogs don't usually bark except at a human intruder. But the kennels are set at a distance and the house is double glazed. A listening system seemed the best security, and it's one which can give me warning even if I'm down in the village or training dogs on The Moss.'

'The intruder was probably somebody who was known to the dogs?' the Inspector suggested.

I shrugged. Beth's earlier comment suddenly made sense. 'Not necessarily,' I said. 'He was in the isolation kennel, which is well away from the others.'

'Samson wouldn't have cared who went near him,' Beth said. 'He was feeling too sorry for himself. But the breeze is blowing from the isolation kennel towards the others. However quietly he walked, I think the dogs would have scented a stranger.'

'With this result,' I said. The loudspeakers were still relaying the barking of many agitated dogs. Beth got up and turned the volume down.

There was a moment of uncomfortable silence. Few visitors would be known to the majority of the dogs. When the Inspector pressed me, I was unable to be sure of anybody other than ourselves who could approach the kennels without setting off a chain reaction.

'And you three were together all the time?' the Inspector asked.

'Definitely,' Henry said.

Beth was asking Isobel a question. I thought that she was trying to lead the conversation away from dangerous ground. 'Did the wrong-number phone call happen before or after you went out to look at Samson?' she asked.

'About five minutes after,' Isobel said.

'But what on earth has that got to do with anything?' I asked.

'Probably nothing,' Beth said. She studied my face for a few seconds. 'And now, I think that you should go to bed. He's not been very well,' she explained.

The Inspector looked at me and nodded. 'There will be more questions,' he said, 'but they can wait. I'm glad your dog's going to be all right. We'll want to look the place over in daylight. Try not to disturb the scene until then.'

'We'll have to be at work early,' Isobel said. 'These are animals, not objects. We have young puppies to feed. We'll leave the isolation kennel alone for the moment.'

'My men will be here at first light,' the Inspector said.

On my way to bed, I visited Samson. He lay as limp as a discarded sweater along the table but his breathing looked good. I rubbed his head. It was odd that the snub-nosed working springers so often had the best noses for scenting game. I wondered what the chances might be of breeding a dog with the looks of Ben and the talent of Samson and decided that they were not good. When you mix blood-lines, too often you get the worst instead of the best of both, which is why dual champions are less common than misshapen dunces. Beauty and brains seldom go together.

The thought put me in mind of Beth. Thinking of her, I hauled myself up the stairs.

Dawn was no more than a distant paleness out over the North Sea when I came downstairs again. I wanted to sleep for another hour, a week, for ever, but sleep was

129

evasive. When I heard Beth creep downstairs, it escaped altogether. I dressed and followed her down.

The percolator was bubbling in an empty kitchen. I found Beth in Isobel's surgery. Samson was awake and feeling, if anything, worse than I did. He had vomited again in the night although he had nothing left but slime to bring up. Beth was finishing the cleaning up around him.

Around a breeding kennel, there is more to life than playing with pretty puppies. A kennel-maid spends much of her time disposing of canine faeces and worse. But Beth never complained. She adjusted the diet to keep faeces firm and moist and then got on with a duty which I, for one, was happy to leave to her whenever I could. 'He's on the mend,' she said cheerfully, wringing out a cloth into a bucket. 'I think he was trying to tell me that he's hungry. Nothing for you, old fellow, until Mrs Kitts says so.'

'Join the club,' I told him and he nibbled gently at my hand.

'You belong to a different club,' Beth said, grinning at me. 'You can have as much breakfast as you're prepared to eat. There, that's finished until the next time. Come along. No, not you, Greedy Guts,' she added. Samson gave up trying to follow us through to the kitchen.

She sat me at the kitchen table and put cereal in front of me while she put on water to boil.

'What do you think is really going on around here?' she asked me.

I knew that she was only trying to keep my mind off the poorness of my appetite but I went along with the game. 'It's not easy to separate reasoning from wishful thinking,' I said. 'What I'd prefer would be that somebody borrowed Ian West's pump-up air rifle and pinched a bullet from Joe Little's car.'

'But that wouldn't make sense of your adaptor being taken and returned,' she said.

'It requires something more complicated in the way of explanations.' I took another spoonful of cereal. It was going down satisfactorily and staying there. 'Imagine a conspiracy of two people looking for the means to commit murder. One of them sees my adaptor on the shelf and borrows it on impulse, only to find that he can't get his hands on any cartridges. Meantime, the other has spotted Ian's air rifle and Joe's bullets.'

'In that case,' Beth said thoughtfully, 'why take the risk of returning your adaptor?'

During the dark hours of wakefulness my mind had been picking at these thoughts, unable to leave the scab alone. 'All right then,' I said, 'try this one. Somebody shot her, maybe with his own rifle, possibly on the spur of the moment. The bullet went through her. Say it rebounded off the wall and landed on the path. No point leaving it for the police to match up with his rifling. He slipped it into his pocket. Then he had a bright idea. If he got his hands on my adaptor, fired a bullet through it and put the bullet where the police would find it, he'd have diverted suspicion from himself.'

'To you.'

'One of the three of us, yes.'

For one moment, Beth looked deeply shocked. Then she relaxed. 'I don't buy it,' she said. 'The bullet would have been planted and found by now.'

'Perhaps it has. The police don't tell Henry everything.'

She shook her head. 'Your adaptor went missing on Thursday. Before the murder.'

'We don't know that,' I said. 'It may not be true. We don't know what other opportunities he may have had. Do you never leave somebody in the shop while you go to answer the phone or meet a visitor? I know that I do.'

'If anybody gave him such a chance, it would have been yourself,' Beth pointed out. 'The murder was on Friday evening and it was returned on Saturday evening. Isobel and I were away all that time. Did you leave the shop unlocked?'

'Not that I remember. There were no visitors. On the

other hand ... Who was here the day the shop was unlocked?'

'Thursday?' Beth looked at me, wide-eyed, while she thought. 'Obviously, if somebody had asked for something out of the shop, we'd have noticed that the door was unlocked and locked up again afterwards. Mrs Kitts was going to do some training with Samson and she'd left her usual whistle at home so she went to take another out of stock while you were putting away the blank cartridge pistol you'd been using with the puppies and I was unpacking some books and shampoos and things which had come in that morning,' she said, apparently all in one breath. 'That's how we came to make a muddle of who was to lock up. You went into Dundee for bulk dogfood, Mrs Kitts took Samson to The Moss for training and I was busy getting the kennels and runs clean and then brushing all the dogs.

'Mr Little came looking for Mrs Kitts while she was out and he went off to find her on The Moss. Mr and Mrs Spring drove over to ask me something. But I don't think any of them went near the shop. Of course, anybody who walked up from the village and found it unlocked wouldn't have hung around after pinching your adaptor and a few cartridges.'

'The cartridges were in the gun-safe, and that really was locked,' I said. 'I already told you that.'

For once, Beth let my rebuke go by. 'So he got them from somebody else. Never mind that for the moment. Do we have any idea who the killer is?'

While she removed my empty bowl and put down a boiled egg and toast, I thought about it. It was disquieting to think about my neighbours, some of them my friends, in such a light, and yet once I began I could well envisage any one of them being pushed over the brink. 'We're swamped with motives,' I said. 'She seemed to go out of her way to make everybody hate her. You could never go into the village without hearing stories of a fresh row with somebody.'

132

'That's true.' Beth was taking her own breakfast without sitting down. She was leaning back against the worktop with her legs spread, a posture which showed off her lithe figure to perfection. I was sure that she used this posture deliberately, as another ploy for keeping my mind off my miseries. 'It might even be somebody, or two or three people, that we've never even heard of.'

'I'd be just as happy to think so,' I said.

'But I'll tell you something else that happened,' Beth said. 'It was only last week, just after one of Mrs Cory's bitches was poisoned. I was in the shop and Mrs Daiches met Laurie Duffus in the doorway and made some snide remark. He said something back and she hit the ceiling, called him words I wouldn't have expected her to know. Well, you know Laurie, he isn't easily upset. He's another one who enjoys a good slanging match, but I swear he was white and shaking.'

'What had he said?' I asked, interested in spite of myself. I had never managed to provoke such an explosive reaction.

'I asked him that afterwards. He said that he'd been so annoyed at being spoken to like a peasant who'd got in the way of a queen that he'd accused her of poisoning his ferrets. She'd been going on at him for weeks, telling him to get rid of his ferrets because they were cruel and the smell upset her dogs.'

'Mrs Cory had been telling him the same thing,' I said.

'Well, they were silly. I never knew a dog that was upset by the smell of ferrets, except a Yorkshire terrier once that had been bitten as a puppy. Laurie admitted to me that he thought the two ferrets that died had been his own fault. He thinks he'd given them meat which hadn't quite thawed out from the freezer. He was only looking for something to annoy her.'

'He seems to have succeeded.'

I had finished, even managing marmalade on the last scrap of toast. Light was growing outside the window and

I could hear footsteps outside. One of the dogs began to bark and set off another. I felt in no hurry to go out and begin the day by meeting more police. My digestion usually suffered if I moved too quickly after a meal.

'I can't see Mrs Daiches poisoning one of Mrs Cory's dogs,' I said. 'They were the only two who liked each other. Two vitriolic old bitches together. Them against the world, that sort of thing.'

'You may be right.' She took the dishes to the sink and spoke over her shoulder. 'But there must have been something wrong. There was a dog show a week past Saturday and they always went together even if one of them wasn't showing. But Mrs Cory cried off. Forfeited an entrance fee, from what I heard.'

'The end of the world must have been nigh,' I said. Mrs Cory had never been known to waste a penny. 'If my you-know-what was used, the killer must have had a shotgun. Laurie Duffus has a gun, but I've only seen him out with a twenty-bore. Of course, he could have another. Do you fancy him for a murderer? She must have been a damned uncomfortable next-door neighbour and he's always resented our successes at field trials.'

She had completed the washing up. Now that I had finished eating she felt no need to draw out the conversation. 'No,' she said briskly, drying her hands carefully and then anointing them with cream from a jar. Beth's hands were in hot water a hundred times a day but she managed to keep them smooth and soft. 'I don't fancy him for a killer, nor for anything else. He's all mouth and trousers. And I still think that they got too much fun out of slanging each other to spoil it by killing. Come on. We'd better get moving.'

Outside, a sickly sun was just topping the hills. Four constables were searching the vicinity of the isolation pen. The poisoned meat seemed to have disappeared. Isobel arrived, on foot, and hurried inside to visit the sick.

Sergeant Flodden seemed to be in charge and he pounced

on me. 'While we're here,' he said, 'do you mind if we look around?'

I guessed that he was making the attempted poisoning the excuse for an intensive search. To refuse would have been suspicious and I thought that if he did not already have a search warrant he could get one within the hour. Beth, who I could see from the corner of my eye, was not making any negative signals. 'Go anywhere you like,' I said. 'If you want the shop unlocked, just ask. You'll want to see our shoes, to compare them with any footprints you find.'

'Just that sort of thing,' he said. 'I'm very grateful.'

*Like hell*, I said to myself.

The next hour or two must have driven the police to the bounds of their patience. But I forgot all my woes in watching a scene develop which, secretly, I thought hilarious. After the puppies had been fed, all the dogs had to be released onto the grass while the pens were cleaned. These were spaniels, mostly young, all curious and friendly. They could have been released in batches but Beth took a malicious pleasure in turning them all out together. I tried to control them but even when Isobel joined me it was impossible.

There was plenty of lawn but the sight of a group of unfamiliar figures searching through the grass was an irresistible magnet to any dog accustomed to spending its free moments in the same activity. Each constable had to be visited by each dog, most of them leaving a souvenir by way of greeting. Any officer rash enough to bend down for a closer look at some possible clue could expect his face to be well licked. I was constantly being presented with gloves which had been removed while some discarded item, usually an expended blank cartridge, was carefully lifted. (There must have been a thousand of these. The extended garden was spacious enough to allow use of the dummy launcher, with the added advantage that the frequent sound of shots was a useful acclimatisation for young puppies.) The constable who was self-consciously sweeping the garden with a metal detector was never accompanied by less than half a dozen dogs all wanting to play with his toy. When Beth was near, the language was moderated and quiet; but when she moved away, the air was blue.

Training on the lawns was out of the question. When the cleaning out was finished, Beth took the younger dogs to the barn. I was planning to take the senior class to The Moss when the outside bell announced a phone call. Isobel went to answer it but she came out again and waved to me.

'Dr Harper,' she called.

I hurried inside and squeezed into the tiny office between Isobel's filing cabinets. I was out again in two minutes.

'He wants to see me right away,' I told Isobel.

'Don't look so worried,' she said. 'He isn't going to have you put down. It's probably good news.'

'Or false hopes.' I had been had before. 'Will you take the older dogs to The Moss? Test them for weaknesses.'

'You don't want me to keep an eye on our visitors?'

'Don't bother,' I said. 'Let them think we don't know they're looking for weapons. Beth can check that they haven't pinched anything.'

# TWELVE

I walked down to the surgery, taking Ben with me. He came steadily at heel and even sat promptly to the whistle with only occasional reminding. I decided that there might be hope for both of us yet.

The search around the Daiches' house was continuing, the number of officers poking dispiritedly around the gardens and field seeming only slightly depleted by the men now scouring Three Oaks Kennels. The criminals of Kirkcaldy and Burntisland, I decided, had been left to get on with their business.

Dr Harper lived in the village, in the last house at the far end. He was a partner in a large practice in Glenrothes, but kept a consulting room at home where he could at least write prescriptions for the local elderly or infirm. If physical treatment beyond a simple injection was required, one had to travel; but the good doctor, despite his irritable manner, was generous with seats in his own car for those who would otherwise have had to change buses twice to make the single journey.

I hitched Ben to the gatepost and went inside. Dr Harper seated me in a deep, leather armchair in a consulting room which, but for the wash basin and discreetly covered trolley in the corner, would more nearly have resembled a segment of an old-fashioned club.

'Some progress at last,' he said. 'Those last blood samples for the London School of Tropical Medicine produced the clue. Apparently you were set upon by a leech.'

'Dozens of them,' I said. 'I told you that.'

He waved his hand testily. 'One of them seems to have been carrying a rare virus – so rare that it doesn't even have a Latin name, let alone an English one. The natives have a name for it which doesn't translate but which implies that it makes a man feel as if he's got too many importunate wives.'

'That sounds like the right one,' I said. 'How do they treat it?'

'They use a decoction from some foul sub-tropical plant which gives horrific side-effects, sometimes fatal.'

'I think I'd rather stay with the disease,' I said.

He scowled at me ferociously. 'I have a surgery in Glenrothes in less than an hour,' he said. 'If you want to do all the talking, we may as well pack up now and you can come and see me there.'

I said that I was sorry.

'Very well. A doctor in California, one of those dedicated men who put in their vacations giving a medical service in under-developed countries, ran an analysis of the plant and found several natural poisons and hallucinogens alongside the active ingredient. UCLA, on his behalf, tried to purify it but failed. Instead, they synthesised a chemical which approximates closely to that active ingredient. This was tested – if you can call it a test – on the very few cases which have since been discovered, with results that can be considered very satisfactory. A supply reached me this morning via LSTM. The accompanying letter suggests that if, after due consideration of the variables, you want to undergo the treatment, I give you the first injection and you let them study you and review progress in a week or two.'

Rather than be accused of trying to hog the discussion, I nodded and smiled and began to roll up my sleeve.

He snorted but half smiled. 'Before we rush into it, a few words of warning. There would still be a long road to travel, more blood changes, more tests, all the things you've hated, but at the end of that road lies a high probability of a cure. There also lies a high probability of side-effects. At best, these might be no more than the symptoms you're already suffering.'

'And at worst?' I asked.

'We can only guess – for which reason you'd have to sign a disclaimer before I could treat you. But animal testing produced no deaths whatever except at far higher dosages than we would consider giving to a patient and the few human guinea-pigs are still thriving. At worst, I would expect occasional lassitude, perhaps nausea, dizziness, even blackouts. Possibly hallucinations or temporary amnesia. But the side-effects would lessen as treatment progressed.'

He was very solemn. I began to feel a distinct sensation of coldness about the feet. 'You're sure that I wouldn't be being used as another guinea-pig?' I asked.

'Of course you'd be a guinea-pig. Did you think that you could pick up an almost unknown tropical bug and have some pharmacist take down the remedy from the top shelf? You can thank your stars that the necessary animal trials have already been conducted. It can now be tested on human volunteers. That's you, in case you hadn't realised it.'

'Well, would I have to go into hospital again?'

'For anyone else, I would book a bed at Ninewells,' he said. 'Frankly, I think it would be unnecessary, bearing in mind the unlikelihood of any serious effects and the uncertainty as to whether such effects would develop tomorrow or after several months. In your case, you make such a bad patient that I won't even consider it. Even if you did react unfavourably, the only available treatment would be bed-rest. My advice would be, stay at home, stick to a light diet, avoid alcohol except in strictest moderation and try not to be alone.'

I thought of pointing out that I slept alone but held my peace. In the first place, he would probably have retorted that if I blacked out in my bed for a few hours no harm would be done and neither I nor anybody else would be likely to know it. And, in the second place, he might not have believed me.

'Perhaps you'd better go away and think about it,' he said more kindly.

If I thought about it, I knew that I would chicken out. 'Let's get on with it,' I said.

His white eyebrows went up. 'You're sure you understand what you're doing?'

'No, of course I don't,' I said. 'How could I? What would you do, if it were you?' I asked him.

'It wouldn't be me. I'd have more sense than to go wading in swamps among infected leeches.'

'Suppose you'd caught it from a blood transfusion or an infected needle. Would you accept this treatment?'

'Taking such a decision in the face of reality would be quite different from a hypothetical case,' he said. 'But, yes. I think I would.'

'Then it sounds like a reasonable bet,' I said. 'Let's get on with it before I lose my nerve.'

He only nodded. The old devil had known what I would decide before he had even posed the question. 'We start with a single injection. They'll want you down in London for tests in ten days,' he said, 'or, if you've had a bad reaction, as soon after that as you're fit to travel. But first, you'd better read this and sign.'

I signed without reading. If the stuff killed me, I would hardly be in a position to sue anybody.

Ten minutes later, I was back in the street. Ben seemed relieved to see me. As we walked back, I explored my own senses, wondering whether I felt better or was about to go on a trip. To my surprise, I felt no different despite the presence of something alien in my bloodstream which might restore my health or knock me flat. But although dark clouds had closed in overhead I had a persistent delusion that the sun was still shining. Was that, I wondered, the first hallucination? Or the beginning of a light at the end of the tunnel?

In a mood which combined hope and fear, I wanted to give somebody a present. I had not been vary amiable to Beth – indeed, I was hard put to it to remember the last time that I had addressed a kind word to her although she was eternally catering to my needs. She was a good girl. I was nearing the shop. Beth had a sweet tooth. A large box of chocolates might begin to redress the balance.

Ben sat obediently while I entered the shop. Ian West was serving one of the local womenfolk. When she left, we had the place to ourselves. I had used the time to pick out the best from his modest selection of chocolates.

While he made change we swapped a few banal remarks about the weather. He seemed depressed; remarks about his airgun or my state of health would have seemed equally inapposite. He was handing me my purchase when I heard him gasp. I followed his eyes. Ben had followed me into the shop when the earlier customer opened the door and was standing, looking expectantly at Ian with his tail slowly waving. Dogs often get to know that a shopkeeper is a soft touch.

'My God!' Ian said. His voice was shaking. 'For a moment, I could have sworn that it was Andy.'

'What about Andy?' I asked. I remembered, too late, that I had not seen Ian's spaniel around for several weeks. And somebody had said something about Mrs Cory having 'sold him a pup'.

'Andy . . . had to be put down,' Ian said. He turned away and became very busy with his shelves.

'I'm so sorry,' I said. 'I know how it is.' And I got out of there as quickly as I could. There are times when words are worse than nothing.

I had made up my mind to be evasive with Beth and Isobel unless and until circumstances forced me to be frank. We had had too many disappointments in the past and they would only have fussed. It was enough that I now had a chance of a normal life instead of only being fit to drift with the current. Some people are born to be passengers in life, but I preferred to be its captain.

In the event, the ladies were denied the opportunity to batter me with their questions. Sergeant Flodden was waiting for me on my return home. I took him into the sitting room and Ben came along with us, off the leash and beautifully to heel. There were signs that the room had been searched, but everything had been restored to comparative tidiness. Sounds of further searching came down through the ceiling.

The Sergeant sat and rested his notebook on his knee. His air, as usual, was maddeningly self-sufficient. Outside, the rain had started. The room was unusually dark. I switched on the lights before I sat down. The room looked cheerful and familiar again.

'Have you found out anything useful?' I asked.

He hesitated. 'About the attempted poisoning? Slug pellets, as you suggested, and a popular brand at that, tucked into a nice piece of steak. The lab says that the steak had been frozen at one time, which may or may not be of help – always assuming that the dog-poisoning has anything to do with the crime.'

'Poisoning somebody else's dog is surely a crime in its own right,' I pointed out.

'Yes, of course.' His voice suggested that it was a very much lesser crime than murder. 'Almost every house around here has a freezer.'

'You need one in the country. As far as I know, the Springs are the only vegetarians around here, if that's any help,' I added.

He thanked me and made a note of it, although I had the impression that he knew it already. 'There were too many faint footprints around for us to make anything of them, and if the poisoner brought the steak in a box or a bag he took it away again with him.'

'In other words, nothing,' I said.

'You could say so. But there was something else I wanted to ask you about.'

'Go ahead and ask.' I braced myself. Then I realised that he was watching me intently and I tried to relax my muscles. Ben must have sensed something. He sat up and nosed my hand, giving me an excuse to shift my position as I patted him.

'We have been informed that you have an adaptor enabling small-bore ammunition to be fired through a shotgun.'

So there it was. I wished that Beth were there, if only to furnish moral support. If the Sergeant had known it, he could probably have got all that he wanted from me by means of a little gentle persuasion and the granting of some time for thought. By trying to push me, he was inducing an equal and opposite reaction. Like Beth, I decided not to lie if it could be avoided. 'And just who gave you that supposed piece of information?' I asked.

'I'm not in a position to tell you that,' he said. He tacked on one of his very rare Sirs as an afterthought.

'Then I don't feel obliged to comment,' I said. 'I've given you every possible facility for looking around. Did you find such a thing about the place?'

'Not yet. Your partner let us into the shop, but she didn't have a key to your gun-safe.'

'You've already seen inside my gun-safe,' I said.

'Something might well have been locked away in it since then.'

I sighed, probably overdoing it, and gave him the gun-safe key. 'I suppose it's your job to be suspicious,' I said.

The Sergeant permitted himself a faint smile. 'When we're suspicious, you'll know it,' he said. 'At the moment, we're at the stage of gathering every fact that we can. So, of course, we have to follow up every statement.'

There was a slight hesitation in there somewhere. I decided that I had found a chink worth hammering a wedge into. 'A statement from whom?'

'That is not the sort of information that we divulge.' His voice, I thought, was very slightly defensive.

'You'll divulge it soon enough if you repeat any such allegation in court,' I said.

He locked eyes with me. I tried to match his self-confidence. The Sergeant suddenly became more human. 'If I wanted to tell you,' he said, 'I couldn't. The information came in the form of an anonymous letter.'

'Did it, by God!' I said, although the news hardly came as a surprise. Beth, I remembered, had predicted something of the sort.

'We've had a spate of them,' the Sergeant said. 'All apparently from the same source. Ruled capitals on plain typing paper. No fingerprints. We don't usually like acting on anonymous letters. But very accurate most of the information has proved. Not always relevant, but accurate. Until now.'

'As accurate as the information that Henry Kitts had an off-certificate rifle?' I asked him.

He had the grace to smile, more openly this time, and to unbend a little more. 'You know about that little fiasco, do you? Well, I suppose you would, Mr Kitts being your partner's husband. As far as we know, that particular information was incorrect. But his air rifle looks very much like a firearm. It would be an easy mistake to make.'

'Come off it,' I said. 'Anybody who knew about guns could tell the difference.'

'Our letter-writer may not be an expert on guns—'

'In which case,' I said, 'your letter-writer may have confused my blank cartridge adaptor with a rifle adaptor.'

'That might be possible,' he said. He was his stiff and uncompromising self again. 'On the other hand, the letter-writer may merely have had a grudge against Mr Kitts.'

'And against me.'

'The paper is exactly the same as that in your office.'

I saw what he was getting at and I did not like it. I thought of asking him why I might have a grudge against

Henry, but Henry's tactless remarks in the hotel might well have been overheard. The subject was better avoided. 'That paper's almost universal,' I said. 'And I certainly wouldn't accuse myself of anything.'

'They usually do. Whenever we get a series of anonymous letters, the writer almost always turns out to have sent one to himself – or herself – as a blind. They think they're being very clever. Nine times out of ten, the recipient of the least damaging letter is also the poison pen. You're sure you don't want to make any comment?'

He seemed to be admitting that the letter about my adaptor was the least damaging, but I had a mad thought that it might be necessary to produce the adaptor in order to prove that I was not a writer of anonymous letters. I pushed it aside. 'The comment I'd like to make,' I said, 'would curl your ears. If you're paying attention to anonymous letters, I don't feel inclined to make any more comments until I've seen . . . '

'Your solicitor?'

'Hardly,' I said. 'Jim Daiches has been my solicitor ever since I came here. But I could hardly consult him about a matter touching on his wife's murder, now could I?'

The Sergeant thought it over. 'That would take more than a touch of brass neck,' he said. 'No, I suppose you couldn't.'

'I'll find another solicitor if and when it seems necessary,' I said. 'Until then I'll give you any help I can, short of commenting on the outpourings of anonymous letter-writers.'

Sergeant Flodden looked at me placidly for a few seconds and then got to his feet. 'You could always ask Mr Daiches to recommend another solicitor,' he said. 'When it seems necessary, of course. I believe he intends to come and see you on another matter this afternoon. You could ask him then.'

He walked out of the room, leaving me quite as shaken as he had intended.

# THIRTEEN

The Sergeant had departed, no doubt to report my stubborn refusal to fall on his neck and make a tearful confession, but the place still seemed to be infested with policemen. We tried to ignore them. Beth, who, out of the goodness of her heart, had been providing them with tea for most of the morning, called me for lunch. I told her that I was supposed to go onto a light diet. She sniffed and said that I never took anything else. She seemed to have accepted that my visit to the doctor had been routine; but a gift of chocolates might have set her thinking so I hid them in a drawer.

The rain had set in. I could have gone for a training walk with a few of the dogs, but I was taking seriously Dr Harper's admonition about not being alone. Also, I had no wish to land Beth with a handful of wet and muddy spaniels to dry and brush. Instead, I took several dogs at a time into the barn for exercises suited to their stages of training. If I blacked out, I thought that one of them would surely have the sense to go for help, or at least to bark until somebody came.

I finished the afternoon session with the advanced class. I had them seated around me and four dummies were out in the piles of straw in the four corners of the barn when I became aware of the shadow of a figure from the bright doorway. It was not the time to be distracted, when temptation was high and a breach of discipline might set training back a week. I sent the dogs, one at a time by name, for the

146

dummies in random order and seated the dogs again before looking round.

Jim Daiches was standing there in a wet, waxproofed coat, dark suit and black tie, upright in the middle of the doorway as though it would be disrespectful for a newly-made widower to lean against the doorpost. His round face was solemn and even his moustache seemed to droop in mourning, but his stance was firm and I would have hesitated before calling him a broken man.

'Very impressive,' he said. 'Laura's beauty queens can't do more than pose elegantly wherever they're put.'

I told the dogs to stay and went to him, choosing my words carefully as I went. 'You have my sympathy,' I said, which was no more than the truth. 'You must be having a hard time.'

He shrugged. 'Everyone's being very kind,' he said. 'Well, perhaps that's overstating it. The police are monitoring my phone but in their heavy-handed way they're trying not to make life impossible. They've been passing on sympathetic messages. The Corys have been helpful. I haven't seen any-one else until now, but there have been some conventional letters of sympathy through the door. I'm hoping that you can be another friend and help me out.'

'If I possibly can,' I said. 'I was going to call but I decided that you'd have your hands full. Go into the house. If you see Beth, ask her to bring tea or something into the sitting room. Or help yourself to a drink if you fancy it.'

'Tea would do,' he said. His smile was hardly more than a twitch of the muscles around his eyes. 'The Corys seem to be conspiring with the police to make me into an alcoholic. I'm a one-pint man, as you know, but every time I turn around somebody's offering me another glass of medicinal brandy. My own brandy, of course.'

Either the police had finished with the garden or the rain had driven them indoors. I kennelled the dogs, hung up my coat near the kitchen boiler and joined Jim who was pacing around in the sitting room. Samson was curled up on the hearth-rug, taking full advantage of his status as an invalid and never bothering to move even when Jim had to step over him on every circuit.

Jim sat down – reluctantly, I thought, as though his mood was restive. 'You were right,' he said. 'It is hard. Laura . . . wasn't always easy to live with, but she'd been a part of my life for more than twenty years. And you never quite forget the early days. You wouldn't want to. Even as somebody ages, you can still see through the older flesh to an image of what they once were. I suppose we were both very different people then, very close, very wrapped up in each other. Perhaps if I'd made a better job of being a husband she might have stayed the tender person that she used to be.' He paused and looked at the ceiling, too proud to wipe his eyes. 'Nobody should have to go like that,' he said.

I crossed to the window and looked out at the rain. 'What will you do now?' I asked him.

'Take a break, as soon as the police say that I can. And then pick up the threads again. I wanted to speak to you about the dogs.' I heard him blow his nose. When I turned round, he had himself in hand. 'I'm sorry,' he said with a twisted smile. 'I didn't intend any displays of embarrassing emotion. I was going to be firm and businesslike. But when Beth offered her sympathy just now she was so sincere and . . . and sweet that it all came home to me. That's a fine girl you've got there.'

'I know it,' I said.

Nobody had found time to clear out the fireplace. Housework was not really a part of Beth's duties; she had just taken it over as she did everything else – willingly, neatly and unasked. But that day had been different from any other. I laid a new fire over the ashes of the old and lit it.

Beth brought in the tea-trolley. I noticed the third cup, but when she had given us tea and put biscuits where we could reach them she made for the door.

'Stay and join us,' I said. 'Mr Daiches wants to talk dogs. This may affect you.'

Beth poured tea for herself and sat down, knees neatly together, in one of the wing-chairs.

'It's this way,' Jim said. 'I feel like getting away for a few weeks. Abroad, perhaps.'

'Well, you would,' Beth said.

Jim nodded. 'Just to get Christmas and the New Year over. I don't think that I could face that empty house over the season. Laura always enjoyed Christmas. She never did much about it, but she enjoyed it.

'Her dogs are the problem. I never was very taken with show springers – all bounce and no brains. Olive Cory wants to buy them on easy terms, which would suit me very well, but she'll have to put up some more kennel-space. That entails moving one of the kennels she's got and rearranging the runs. The Springs' kennels are full up, what with people going off for winter breaks. Could you take them until, say, mid-January?'

'How many are there now?' I asked. 'Four bitches, is it?'

'Three, but one of them's still nursing a litter of young pups.'

I looked at Beth. 'Could we manage?'

'Difficult, until we can get the isolation kennel scrubbed and fumigated,' she said. I saw her lips moving as she assessed the allocation of kennels in her mind. 'With some doubling-up of the older dogs and if we keep Samson in the house, we could do it. We've had a case of gastro-enteritis,' she told Jim. 'Not serious and we seem to have stopped it at once, but it might be dangerous for young puppies.'

'I heard that you had Samson isolated,' Jim said. 'I'm glad it's nothing much. If I can persuade the Springs to take the nursing bitch and her litter, will you take the other two?'

Beth raised her eyebrows at me.

'Until mid-January,' I said, 'and no longer. We have another litter due then, and God knows how many dogs will come in for retraining when the shooting season's over and the owners want to get away and forget about all the chasing and running-in that's been going unchecked.'

'I'll phone Mrs Spring for you,' Beth said. 'Leave it to me. She won't want to be disobliging. She'll want us to help out with her overflow again in the summer.'

Jim blew out a breath of relief. 'Olive Cory will have space by then. Neill can do the work for her during the Christmas break. After all, he is in property.' He let us see, by a sketch of a smile, that he was joking and then became serious again. 'One other thing. I've agreed with Olive that she can have the dogs on a valuation. She wants the valuer to be one of the show-dog people, but I don't know which of them are her lifelong buddies and while I don't mind doing her a favour I've no intention of being rooked. Would you or Isobel do a valuation for us? Olive would accept it, because she'd expect you to put a low price on show-dogs, but I know that Isobel keeps tabs on prices as well as pedigrees.'

'We could do that,' I said. 'Leave the pedigrees along with the inoculation certificates when you bring the dogs up. Don't make it too soon. We need to re-organise a bit.'

He nodded. 'I'll leave it as long as I can,' he said, 'I've been keeping them cleaned and fed – you'd better sell me another bag of meal before I go. I don't feel up to dog-walking under all those curious eyes just yet, but Olive's taken them out for me several times and one of the young constables has been very helpful.'

There was an awkward silence. He was bottling something up and I was wondering what on earth else one could say to a widower in the circumstances.

Beth cleared her throat. 'I was wondering whether the police told you— ?' she began.

Her attempt at a question seemed to uncork a bottle of effervescent ire. 'The police have been kind and well meaning and they don't tell me a damn thing,' he said, with all the irritation to be expected of one who, as a solicitor, was used to having the police come to heel at his whistle. 'Not even an indication of when I might be able to go away. You'd think that they could at least let me know whether they're making any progress. The other reason that I've avoided facing any neighbours other than the Corys – until this moment – is that I wouldn't know whether I was speaking to the man who'd murdered my wife.'

He caught my glance of surprise. 'I don't mean you, my dear chap,' he said quickly. 'I know you didn't agree with her about spaniels – and, frankly, I was on your side although I wouldn't have dared to say so – but at least the two of you got it out of your systems by slandering each other's dogs in the public bar whenever you met, making the fullest use of irony, sarcasm and rhetoric. I wish I'd caught some of your debates on tape. Once – the time when you said that her dogs were so thick that they thought a whistle was only a sign of admiration and she said that your dogs had no grounds for making such a mistake – I thought that you were both going to give in and laugh, except that you were each forcing an awful scowl at the time. That was the latterday Laura as I'd like to remember her, impassioned by enthusiasm. But it wasn't the sort of conflict that leads to violence.'

'What is?' I asked him.

'God knows,' he said. 'But I've defended enough people on assault charges – and very unlikely people, some of them – to know that, unless the attacker's unbalanced or criminal, the disagreement has to go beyond words or be between people who aren't articulate enough to use words for an outlet. That's what's getting to me. Laura squabbled with everybody, that's how she "got her kicks" as they say. It didn't mean anything.'

'Mrs Cory's just the same,' Beth said. 'Perhaps that's why they got on so well together.'

That struck me as being another silly remark because, while Mrs Cory was subject to a venomous temper, the outbursts of Mrs Daiches had always seemed more cerebral. I had sometimes suspected that she made a calculated choice of occasions on which to let her temper explode.

Jim Daiches relaxed in his chair and sipped at a cup of tea which could have been no more than luke-warm. The fire had burned high, the room was cheerful and he was talking in the abstract instead of from personal grief. 'That came into it,' he said. 'But they'd been friends a long time. Years ago, when our marriages were young, Neill Cory and I clubbed together to rent a small shoot. It was no great shakes, but we worked at it, released a few pheasants, controlled the predators and persuaded the farmer to leave some cover where the partridges could breed. We had a working spaniel apiece. We were our own keepers and trainers and we had a lot of fun. They were the good days.

'Our wives used to come along and beat for us or help with the dog-work. I can't pretend that they were enthusiastic, but it was the fashion for a wife to try to share her husband's interests. We were all younger then. Either of them could have a sharp tongue when crossed – Olive particularly – but we got along.

'The beginning of the end was when I shot a hare and the dog brought it to Laura. I hadn't killed it clean and it was squealing. You know how they squeal.'

'I know,' I said. The cry of a wounded hare can sound distressingly human.

If he heard me he made no sign. He was lost in the past. There were tears, unashamed tears this time, on his cheeks. 'She couldn't bring herself to kill it and by the time I got to her the damage was done. I tried to reason with her, to rationalise, to persuade, but it was no good. She could never even bear to see me go out with a gun again and she brought Olive round to her own way of thinking.

'Things were never the same again. In the end, we gave up the shoot. Neill continued to go after pigeon and rabbits wherever he could get permission, but Laura nagged at me until I gave it up altogether. And our two wives turned against working springers and started to breed for show. The honeymoon was over. Laura would never see that I'd paid her a high compliment, because what I'd given up for her sake had been my sole interest outside of the office. If she could have brought herself to admit . . . But never mind that. Soon, our marriage was companionship and nothing more and Laura's tongue developed its razor-edge. Perhaps it was all my fault. I just don't know.'

He fell silent. He used his handkerchief and held out his cup for a refill.

Beth poured. 'I think that's very sad,' she said. 'But your wife and Mrs Cory stayed friends to the end?'

Jim frowned. His mind was still far away. 'I think so,' he said. 'But, just for the last week or so, there was some tension that I couldn't put my finger on. Nothing was said in my hearing, but I hardly remember them speaking a word to each other except for the exchange of a few platitudes if they met in company. Yet until then they'd been on the phone or popping into each other's houses constantly, for years. I wouldn't like to think of Laura dying without any real friends, but I have a chill feeling that something was wrong.'

'And you don't know what set it off?' Beth asked.

'I've asked Olive. At first, she said that I was imagining things. I was sure that I wasn't, though. When I persisted she said that Laura had been irritated because she – Olive – had been nagging her to get on with making a statement in connection with the lawsuit. You know about the sheep-worrying episode?'

'I was on the spot a few seconds later,' I said.

'So you were.' Jim looked at me for a few seconds. But his awareness faded again. 'I think that any tension dated from a visitor Olive had about ten days ago. I was just arriving home from the office. There was a car at the Corys' gate and a woman was arguing with Olive. Laura was there and seemed to be taking the other woman's side in the argument. Nothing could have been more calculated to set Olive's back up – she always expects a friend to back her, and never mind what the truth may be.

'I couldn't hear what was being said and I was just as happy to put the car in the garage and slip into the house. When Olive gets into an argument, she has a habit of dragging me into it and saying that I'm her solicitor, although I'm not and wouldn't want to be. I have no objection to litigious clients,' he explained to me. I had become real again. 'My livelihood depends on them. But I can do without clients who embark on lawsuits that they're bound to lose, against the best advice.'

I was finding Jim's revelations rather embarrassing but I could hardly cut him short. The loan of an ear seemed to be the least that one could offer a friend in time of stress. But I was feeling lethargic and hoped that he would soon leave. 'You and Neill could go back to your old ways,' I said. 'Will you get a gun again?'

He looked more cheerful. 'I still have my gun,' he said. 'A nice little Churchill Twenty-five, side by side, the only gun I ever shot well with. Laura didn't know. I told her I'd sold it. But I had it well greased and hidden away behind a wardrobe. It was an old friend and I didn't feel like parting with it. I've been taking it out for a clean every week or two, when Laura was out, for old times' sake. With all that waxing and no use, the stock's come up like a mirror.'

I felt wide awake again. 'The police will have found it,' I said. 'They must have searched the place.'

'Must have done. I wonder why they haven't mentioned it. But it doesn't matter. I've kept up my certificate.' He saw that I was looking concerned. 'What's the matter?'

Almost any wording could be dangerous and yet he had to be warned. 'The police were asking me, this morning, whether I had ever had a two-two rifle adaptor to fit a twelve-bore shotgun,' I said cautiously. 'So a carefully hidden shotgun might . . . Well, let's just say that it might send them up a blind alley.'

'They think . . . ?' he began. 'Good Lord! That explains why they keep fobbing me off by telling me they'll know more when they find the bullet. Yes, this could be bloody awkward. You see, long ago I applied for an adaptor on my firearms certificate. I never actually bought it; somebody who'd had one told me that they were inaccurate. But that was before records were computerised. They'll still have the details of my certificate on file but I don't suppose that I could prove that I never bought one.' He fell silent and I saw his face go from white to dull red. Suddenly to see oneself as a murder suspect must come as a jolt, especially to a man who has seen the law from the safe side.

'Who told you that they were inaccurate?' Beth asked.

'I think it was Neill,' Jim said. 'Yes, I remember now. He had one. It was a long time ago. I was with him when he traded it in against a new gun.' He sighed and stretched himself. 'Well, I'd better go home and face the police and a dead house. I think that that's the real reason that this is my first venture out – I couldn't face the thought of going back, expecting someone, finding somebody else in a house which isn't like my home any more. I must face the fact that I'm alone now. I've been alone for years, really, but now I know it.'

# FOURTEEN

I gave Jim his kennel-meal and saw him to his car. He insisted on paying me and I knew that he would have felt insulted if I had refused to take his money. Beth, when I returned, was washing the cups. She could never bear to leave dishes in the sink although she never objected when I did so. I lowered myself carefully into one of the kitchen fireside chairs. My knees, which had once been fit to carry me on a yomp over the high ground to Stanley, seemed to have been replaced by chewed string.

'You do ask people the damnedest questions,' I said.

Beth flushed. 'Well, I'm interested. I've phoned the Springs,' she said over her shoulder. 'They can take the bitch and pups.'

Mention of Mr and Mrs Spring reminded me. 'What did the Springs want when they came up on Thursday?'

'It was nothing for you to worry about.'

'But what was it?' I asked.

'They wanted to ask me whether I'd like a job with them. I told them that I was perfectly happy where I was.'

'Truly?'

'Yes,' she said. 'Truly.'

Silence was punctuated by the clatter of dishes. Remembering the chocolates, I got up and fetched them. 'This is a present,' I said. 'I don't always mean to snap at you.'

She stood, looking down at the prettiness on the lid, for what seemed an hour. 'You can snap if you want to,' she said at last. 'If it makes you feel better. I know you're worried.'

I lowered myself back into the chair. 'I'm worried all right. We're going to have to come clean.'

Beth took a hard look at my face. 'Not yet,' she said. 'It wouldn't do them much good until they find the bullet.'

'They may never find the bloody bullet,' I said fretfully. 'The damn things can come out in the most extraordinary directions. And it's been raining cats and dogs today. Stones float up through earth in wet weather but anything heavier than the soil goes on down.'

'Don't do anything in a hurry,' Beth said. 'The police won't give up. They never do, after a murder. If the pathologist found a trace of lead, she was shot with a bullet, not with an icicle or something, as in the mystery stories. They'll find it if they have to sieve every square yard of soil for half a mile around. And when they find it,' she said, 'they may find that it's been fired from something quite different.'

'You don't really think that,' I said.

'It doesn't seem very likely. But I don't know. And you don't know either,' she said severely. 'You said yourself— '

'I was talking balls as usual.'

'If you weren't then, you are now,' she said. 'It'd be a shame if you went to the police, in sackcloth and ashes and beating your breast and with a rope round your neck like the buggers of Calais— '

'Burghers,' I corrected her.

' — that's what I said – and then to find that she was shot from something quite different.'

I wanted to be convinced but reason was against me. 'Even if the bullet never turns up, there was speckling in the bore of the adaptor. It could tell a forensic scientist a lot about the cartridge. Given the weapon and the story of its going and coming, they could make a good case against a guilty party.'

'Or against you,' she said. 'Or somebody else quite innocent. We've stuck our necks out. Let's keep them out for a little longer. Trust me.'

'A little longer,' I said. 'No more than that. I want to feel like an honest man again.'

'Do you think you'd feel better in the pokey?' she asked. 'You go and do some more training. I'll look after the feeding and cleaning.'

'Where's Isobel?'

'Gone out to show off Oberon's paces to somebody. I think we have a customer.'

'He'd fetch more in the summer,' I said. 'On the other hand, he'd eat most of the extra value between now and then. Mr Symes will be pleased.' I was joking. Mr Symes was the bank manager and he was never pleased.

Before doing anything else, I decided on an experiment. I pulled the bullets from three cartridges and took my air rifle out to the log pile. The bullets flew neither as fast nor as accurately as waisted slugs, but they flew. Through a pump-up air rifle, they would be highly lethal. The remains of the cartridges, I buried.

The rain had been heavy but was now no more than a drizzle. The Moss would be swampland. I took Ben into the barn. He had almost forgotten the lessons which I had drummed into him. We started again from the beginning and even made a little progress. I persevered until I was sure that the lessons were being imprinted, and stopped as soon as I thought that there was a danger of his becoming bored and rebellious. I was back in the kitchen, sitting in one of the fireside chairs and holding onto the arms through an attack of dizziness, when Isobel came in.

She waved a four-figure cheque under my nose. We needed a few dozen cheques like that during the year just to keep going, but the bulk of our sales of trained dogs would come in the summer. Despite what Joe had said, I never failed to be surprised and relieved when purchasers paid up such sums for a trained dog. When you took the value of a puppy and added on the time and feeding needed to bring it to maturity and perfection our prices were not unreasonable, but would-be customers did not always see it that way. Sometimes, one of them would prefer to buy a pup and train it himself, only to bring a confused dog back to me in the hope that I could undo the damage. Those, I overcharged disgracefully and they usually thanked me for it.

Isobel knew of my concern for the dogs' futures. 'The man's a syndicate member, wants to get the dog used to him by next season. Seemed sensible. I think Oboe will be all right there.'

'I'm glad,' I said. I liked Oberon. He was a good dog who had come through his training with flying colours. If he had a fault it was that he over-reacted to correction. A sensible man could be counted on to allow for that. Beth showed much the same sensitivity but I was not always sensible.

The Tuesday was quiet, or at least as quiet as any day ever is around a busy breeding kennel. We had one dogfight, over nothing, necessitating stitches. Ben began to make sustained progress. Samson went back to his kennel. The young dogs seemed inattentive; a year-old bitch turned out to have come suddenly into her first season. Isobel had decided that Samson's enteritis had not been of the infectious sort but, to be safe, we burned a sulphur candle in the isolation kennel and disinfected its run. The police left us alone, to wait and worry.

And public interest in the murder had both attracted the curious and reminded the serious of our existence. We had four sets of visitors who were evidently just browsing, one reporter pretending to be a customer and an aspiring trainer who was looking for a young pup and prepared to pay for it. Man and pup went off happily together, seemingly delighted with each other. The reporter, failing to get a story, wrote a feature about the kennels which was later to bring us enquiries all through the spring. If this went on, we would be able to make a big saving on advertisements.

It was not until the Wednesday that all hell broke loose.

That day also started quietly enough. The pups were fed and the dogs exercised. Isobel and I gave some individual training while Beth cleaned the pens and refilled the water-dishes. Isobel decided that I was off-colour, so she took the advanced class off to The Moss while I taught the juniors on the lawn. Looking back, I believe that I was bored.

After lunch, I gave Ben half an hour to himself. To my surprise he remembered the training of the previous days and seemed to take pleasure in showing it off. He even learned one or two new lessons. I was so pleased that I decided to show his paces before he backslid again.

Isobel was back and catching up with the accounts and other paperwork. She had carried her papers into the kitchen, where she could command more table-space than anywhere else in the house as well as being handy for tea and gossip, but when I entered she was talking earnestly with Beth – about me, I suspected from the silence which fell immediately.

I was too exhilarated to pay attention to what was their usual pattern of behaviour. 'Look at this,' I said. I walked him round the room at heel, sat him and walked away, called him, sent him out again and sat him at a distance. As an encore, he lay down on command. He was responding well to vocal commands but tended to ignore signals.

Beth gave him a round of applause which he seemed to appreciate.

'I'll be damned,' Isobel said. 'He'll never win a field trial, but he'll make somebody an acceptable pet after all. I never thought you'd be able to do anything with the daft beggar.'

She snapped her fingers and Ben went to her, expecting praise and a petting. Isobel produced the miniature torch which was always clipped to her dress and looked deep into his eyes. 'Oh dear!' she said on a falling tone.

Beth's smile was wiped away.

I felt a cold hand grip the back of my neck, the hand of doom. 'He hasn't, has he?' I asked stupidly.

'I'm afraid so. RD,' Isobel said. 'It's at an early stage, but the signs are there. I'll get out my ophthalmoscope later and make sure.'

I felt stunned by the let-down. Retinal dysplasia, along with hip dysplasia and progressive retinal atrophy, is the skeleton at the feast where several of the gundog breeds are concerned. It is a congenital condition and very serious.

'That's an awful shame,' Beth said. 'After all your work. And he's such a beautiful dog. His owners will be heartbroken.'

'Try to say something helpful,' I told her. In my disappointment, I sounded brusquer than I had intended and I saw her flinch. Isobel gave me a small headshake. I wanted to tell Beth that I was sorry but the right words would not come.

Ben looked from one to the other of us with his soulful eyes, wondering why our voices had changed.

'I meant to examine him earlier,' Isobel said, 'but I didn't get around to it. When you gave me his pedigree, I noticed that he had Champion Lucasta of Coneyshaw for a great-granddam. There was RD on both sides of her pedigree and it's cropped up with unpleasant regularity in her descendants.'

Ben had come to me for reassurance and I kneaded the back of his neck while I tried to divert my mind from the dark future which faced him – if, indeed, he had any future at all. 'Doesn't Mrs Cory have one of Lucasta's granddaughters?' I asked. 'I seem to remember her shooting her mouth off about having a Supreme Champion in the pedigree.'

'She did,' Isobel said. 'That was Culrosa, the one that got shot. Just as well, if you ask me. Lucasta's granddam also shows up in Culrosa's sire's pedigree so Culrosa got it with both barrels, you might say. Stupidest bit of breeding I ever came across.'

'Are you sure?' Beth asked.

Isobel's chin went up. Any doubt cast on her phenomenal memory for pedigrees always annoyed her. 'About what?'

'Are you sure that Culrosa was shot? I thought that I'd seen her with Mrs Cory since then.'

Isobel relaxed. 'That was probably Dalgetty,' she said. 'They were half-sisters by the same sire and nearly identical. But Dalgetty's dam came from a clear line, so she's probably all right. Or she was until she was poisoned. There seems to be a curse on Olive Cory. She's left with the younger bitch which is a full sister of Culrosa. She'd be out of her mind if she bred from her.'

'She bred from Culrosa,' I reminded her.

'All right, so she's out of her mind.'

'I expect you're right,' Beth said thoughtfully. 'But I worked for Mrs Cory for a few weeks before I came here, the time she broke her leg, and— '

There was a knocking at the back door and Henry's voice was raised on the threshold. '"Is there anybody there?" said the traveller, knocking on the shithouse door,' he called as he pushed his way inside. His face, always of a high colour, seemed to have been picked out in tones of scarlet.

Isobel blinked at her husband. 'What on earth have you been drinking?' she enquired, without censure.

Beth, unasked, got up and put coffee on to percolate.

'Beer, mostly, until my bladder capacity was exhausted,' Henry said, flopping into a chair. 'But news and rumour, in roughly equal proportions, were flying around the hotel at lunchtime and I thought I'd hang on until I'd collected most of it.'

'And until the hotel ran out of whisky,' Isobel said.

'Didn't run out,' Henry said. 'Just, Flora wouldn't serve me any more. Anyway, I think I'd got most of it.'

162

'Most of what?' we said together. 'The whisky?' Isobel added.

'The news. Did you know,' Henry said, 'that one of those plastic Coca-Cola bottles makes a dashed good silencer? Neill Cory said so. He was on his way to see somebody so he called at home for lunch and looked in for a drink. He says he used to do it often when he had a little four-ten shotgun. Went poaching at dawn, he said. Jus' a minute,' Henry added. 'Got to have a pee.' He heaved himself up and left the room, with surprising steadiness considering his condition.

'But would that work with a two–two rifle bullet?' Beth asked me.

'I'm sure it would,' I said. 'You'd hardly hear a sound if he used the subsonic cartridges.'

'The what?'

'Low-velocity. The ones which don't break the sound barrier. They're quiet to start off with. Even the noise of the high-velocity cartridges would be damped down.'

Beth pointed a finger at me. I half expected her to say Bang! 'That's why a shot wasn't heard,' she said. 'And why the police were asking whether Mrs Daiches was addicted to Coca-Cola.'

Her deductions were too obvious to require a comment. 'I expect they found a Coke bottle with a hole in the bottom,' I said. 'Probably in somebody's dustbin.'

The pipes hissed as Henry flushed the loo. We heard him coming back. When he was safely back in his chair, Isobel, who had gone back to her accounts, looked up and said, 'What else did you hear?'

'They've found a two–two bullet,' Henry said. 'A bullet, not an airgun slug. The pathologist told them that it had come out at an upward angle, so they started on the roofs. It turned up lodged between two slates. Not the Daiches house. Laurie Duffus's.'

I felt a hollowness inside. 'I suppose it's the right one?' I said. 'Two–two bullets can travel for miles. It could have been there for years, left over from somebody shooting crows.'

Henry shrugged. 'Could be. My information's tenth-hand. But rumour has it that there was still a trace of blood on it. Anyway, it went to the forensic lab for study. Rifling marks, if any, and all that clever stuff.'

'Did you find out anything else?' Isobel asked.

'Oh yes,' Henry said. He winked, looking like an elderly satyr. 'This next snippet has set the tongues wagging. Jim Daiches has been a naughty boy. He's been rolling around with his secretary.'

'I can't say that I'm surprised,' Isobel said. 'The way Laura treated him, she was asking for that sort of trouble.'

'Well, I'm bloody well astonished,' Henry said. 'I've seen the lady. She lives in Auchtermuchty,' he added, winking at me again.

'Not interested,' I said. 'I've seen her too.'

'But Auchtermuchty's conveniently on the way to Edinburgh. It seems they found a shotgun hidden away in the Daiches house. And they're sure that Jim used to have a two-two adaptor for the gun. They think he kept it.'

'But he was in Edinburgh,' Beth said.

'Ah, but was he? When the police checked up, he didn't register for his weekend course until around eight p.m. on the Friday and nobody seemed to remember seeing him around before then. Plenty of time to have killed his wife and driven to Edinburgh. Not my own idea,' Henry added hastily. 'It's what I'm told people think the police are thinking. According to Flora's boyfriend, Jim now admits he took time off to visit his lady-love for a bout of how's-your-father and she backs his story, but then she would, wouldn't she? If she wanted him free to marry her.'

This was terrible. Jim's words and manner had stuck in my mind. I could recall every inflection and I would have sworn that he was telling nothing but the truth. I caught Beth's eye and knew that she felt the same. I wanted to think, but the vagueness was creeping back over my mind.

It was as if my brain had been tarred and feathered.

'Do they have him in . . . ' My mental confusion was increasing. Now, suddenly, I found that the word custody refused to come. ' . . . custard?' was the nearest that I could get to it.

Even Henry, whose tongue was only just within his control, was looking at me oddly. 'He's "helping the police with their enquiries",' Henry said. 'And we all know what that means.'

'We've got to . . . ' My eyes were still locked with Beth's. I found that I was unable to pull them away. Words seemed to have dried up.

Beth seemed to have equal difficulty in breaking off our eye-contact. But she got up suddenly and looked at the ceiling. 'This has gone on long enough,' she said clearly. 'And I'm going to put a stop to it.'

My hearing was also behaving oddly. I could have sworn that she said 'shop' rather than 'stop'. My mind was still playing with the connotations of the words when I blacked out, suddenly and completely.

# FIFTEEN

I think that I came to in near-darkness. Somebody was moving in the room. But my mind was taken up with a macabre dance of disembodied faces. The bed felt comfortable and familiar so that I drifted off to sleep again, but not before Joe Little's square face, wearing an expression far from his usual look of tolerant kindness, had swallowed the other. I could see his hands and he carried a dummy launcher in each of them.

It was full daylight when I woke up although the room was dimmed by drawn curtains. Physically I felt drained, but mentally I was alert although light-headed. Isobel, in a blue dressing-gown, was sitting in the basket-chair, doing her nails. Something heavy was lying across my feet.

'What the hell?' I said.

She jerked her head up, looked at me anxiously and then let a slow smile wash over her face. 'That's my boy,' she said. 'I had a bet with Henry that those would be your first words. How do you feel?'

'I feel much, much better,' I said. I tried to sit up, but the effort was too great. The heavy object on my feet turned out to be Ben. 'What's he doing here?'

'He was more worried than any of us. He refused to come out, so I left him. He couldn't do any harm except perhaps to pass on a flea or two, and he might even do some good. Stroking a furry animal is supposed to be good therapy.'

'Tell me what's been going on.'

'How much do you remember?'

It was a difficult question. If you have forgotten something, how do you know it? 'I think I remember everything up to the moment when Beth said that she was going to do something. I was on the way out at the time and I didn't really understand her. What happened after that?'

'I didn't understand her either,' Isobel said. 'I still don't. After that, you flopped gently forward onto the table. I made you more comfortable and checked that you still had a pulse and weren't choking on your tongue. Beth was already at the phone and screaming for Doc Harper. He was at home. He said he'd told you that a blackout had always been on the cards; but he must have been worried because he made it up here in about three minutes.' Isobel broke off and shook her head at me. 'You young idiot, why didn't you tell us that you were on a new treatment and might flake out, instead of letting us think you'd died all over the kitchen table?'

Trying to watch her face was too great a strain on my neck. I let my head flop in the pillows. 'I didn't want to keep finding the pair of you behind me, waiting for me to fall backwards,' I said.

'Oh yes? Typical! Some people aren't man enough to accept help from women. You think that it impugns your virility, or something. The doctor said that he'd have put you into hospital except that he didn't think they'd have you after the nuisance you made of yourself once before. Beth was getting in a panic at the idea of being left alone with all the dogs plus a moribund employer. She kept using words like coma and Dr Harper kept using longer words which he meant to be reassuring but which made it sound even worse, so I kept translating into veterinary terms which I thought she'd understand more easily. I suppose I made you sound like a puppy with distemper, but it helped to calm her down. Even so I had to agree to stay for a night or two to help out. Henry's sleeping at home but coming here for his meals.

'And talking of meals,' she said, 'I feel like a cup of tea.' She waited, expectantly.

I realised that I had not eaten since lunch on what I presumed to have been the previous day. 'I feel a bit empty,' I said.

She beamed at me. 'Doc said not to force food on you until you asked for it. He said that the worst would be over when you did.'

'I'm asking,' I said. 'But first, tell me. Are the police waiting to interview me?'

'Of course they're not,' she said, pausing in the doorway. 'What could you tell them?'

She vanished before I could answer her or ask any more questions and I was left to puzzle over a thousand conundrums. Ten minutes later, she brought me in a tray of scrambled eggs, toast and tea. The smell drove all anxieties out of my mind. Ben wanted to share my breakfast with me, but my need was the greater.

'I'm still hungry,' I said, swallowing the last of the toast. 'In fact, I'm ravenous.'

'I've been waiting for more than a year to hear you say that,' she said. Something in her voice made me raise my head again. She was blinking hard. 'But it's light diet for you today. You can get up for a little while this afternoon if you feel up to it, and have a full diet tomorrow if you can take it and keep it down.'

I wanted to get up straight away and raid the kitchen, but my limbs still felt like spaghetti. 'Go on telling me what happened,' I said.

'I think I told you most of it.'

'Tell me what Beth did.'

'I'm damned if I know what Beth did,' she said irritably. 'She doesn't communicate very well. I'd have thought that she'd gone off her rocker, except that I know that beneath that silly shell she's really quite bright.'

168

'Is she? She always seems a little dim-witted to me.'

'To you, she would,' Isobel said. 'That's because you persist in terrifying her.'

'Rubbish!' I said. 'Me?'

'Yes, you. She's afraid of making a fool of herself, so, of course, she keeps doing just that. And then you keep putting her down. I think she accepts that you need somebody to let off steam at when you don't feel up to par, but that doesn't help her to feel any better about herself. You should try being nicer to her. In fact,' Isobel said, 'you should marry the girl instead of fooling around with an old trout like me. She adores you, you know.'

I closed my eyes for a few seconds. Perhaps I was hallucinating. But Ben's weight on my legs seemed real enough, and the sound of the basket-chair as Isobel shifted her weight. 'Go on about what she did,' I said at last.

'If you insist. But don't think that we've left the subject behind for ever. Well, after we'd got you to bed and Doc had assured Beth thirty-two times that you were on the road to recovery rather than on your last legs and after we'd convinced her that she wouldn't be doing any good keeping a vigil at your bedside like a sort of cross between Greyfriars Bobby and the saintlier sort of nun – not that that's the sort of hybridisation I'd expect to run true . . .' Isobel lost her train of thought and came to a halt. 'What was I saying?'

'God knows,' I said. 'I'd asked you what Beth did and you started to ramble.' By turning on my side, I found that I was able to watch Isobel's face. Her expression of baffled fury was well worth the effort.

'It was enough to make anybody turn incoherent. She took a new pack of surgical gloves out of my bag, without so much as a by your leave, and went into the office with them for about twenty minutes. And I know that the office isn't exactly clean and tidy,' Isobel said, 'but you don't have to put gloves on to go inside unless you're unduly fastidious.

'When she appeared in the kitchen again, she had her coat on and there was a long envelope sticking out of the pocket. She gave me back my gloves, for all the good they'll be to me when she wouldn't even say what she'd been doing in them. And then she went over to the central heating boiler and started tearing it to pieces with her bare hands.'

I assumed that my ears were not playing tricks on me again. 'She really must have lost her marbles,' I said. 'You were right the first time.'

'That's what I thought. But what she actually did was to jerk out a piece of pipe. I looked at it after she'd gone. You remember how the boiler stands out a bit from the wall, with three or four pipes going back through the wall to the cylinder on the other side? Well, this was a piece of copper pipe cut to just the right length to jam between the back of the boiler and the wall. When I tried it back in place, it looked as if it had been there since the heating was installed. She slipped something out of it and put it in her other pocket. And then she went out.'

'Without saying anything?' I asked.

Isobel's knuckles whitened in exasperation. 'She said quite a lot, but not a damn thing that made sense. And she wouldn't answer any direct questions at all, she just shook her head and uttered some more gibberish. Most of the time, she seemed to be talking to herself. She said something about two playing at that game and sometimes one had to bury the truth to bring it out. And more than once she said that she hoped that she was doing the right thing. Then she said that it was too early and she'd feed the dogs before she went.

'She fed Samson in the kitchen before bedding him down in the surgery. He's taking his food now, you'll be glad to hear. And she said a funny thing to him. She patted him and said that he was a good dog but an even better clue. I *think* she said "clue". Then she wheeled out the trolley with the feed for all the dogs. She said that she didn't want any help. I could hear her for some time, over the loudspeakers, working away and talking to the dogs. I think she told the bastards more than she'd ever told me! Then it stopped and she seemed to vanish quietly away.

'She stayed out for most of the night. I got up to take a look at you at about four this morning and she had just come in. She was giving her shoes a careful clean and polish, of all things! All she'd say was that she thought everything would be all right now.'

'Poor kid, she must be exhausted,' I said.

'She's up again. In fact, I'd better put some clothes on and go and help her with the chores. You'll be all right on your own?'

'I want to see her,' I said.

'Well, you'll just have to wait. When the feeding and cleaning and exercise are done, I'm going to send her back to bed.'

She left me alone. I kicked Ben off and tried to exercise a little strength back into my legs and arms. But I surprised myself by waking up again to find that the morning was gone and Isobel had brought me up another tray. Boiled fish, this time, with mashed potatoes and spinach. The curtains were drawn back and sunshine had returned.

The first I saw of Beth was when I managed to dress myself and totter down the stairs. Ben followed at my heel, solicitous as any nurse.

I met Beth in the hall. She looked ready to turn and flee, but then she faced me – defiantly, I thought. I was about to pour out a dozen questions when I heard Isobel hang up the phone and a moment later she came out of the office.

'For God's sake!' Isobel said furiously. 'No wonder they don't want you back in hospital! I told you that I was coming up for you.'

'And now you don't have to,' I retorted. It sounded brave but I spoiled it by having to grab her arm.

I turned towards the kitchen but Isobel herded me into the sitting room. 'You're going to have visitors, if you feel up to it.'

'The police?' I asked.

She snorted and looked up at the ceiling. Evidently, being plagued by idiots was as much as she could bear. 'In Heaven's name stop going on about the police,' she snapped. 'Beth's given Henry his lunch and there's . . . somebody else coming.'

'Who?'

'I'll tell you later. Sit down here. Henry's got more news. He's all choked up with it but he won't say anything until we're all together. He says he's damned if he's going to tell the same story and be asked the same questions over and over.'

Beth's eyes were sending me messages which I was quite unable to interpret. Her face showed tiredness and possibly strain. I desperately wanted a word alone with her, but Henry and Isobel decided to take coffee with us and although I trusted their discretion I had no intention of burdening them with secrets – if, indeed, we still had any secrets, which was what I was most desperate to find out.

They made me feel a hundred years old by settling me on the settee with a rug over my knees and a cup of weak tea in my hand. I remembered my grandmother, in her declining years, being treated similarly and on the same settee, although it had then been covered in faded brocade. I accepted the coddling with as much grace as I could manage. Argument would only have taken up more time and I urgently wanted to know whether our troubles were over or only just beginning. The sunshine beyond the windows was a cold light, but the fire had been lit and the room was as comforting as a childhood nursery.

'Now,' Isobel said to Henry. 'What have you found out?'

'Big doings,' Henry said complacently. 'I called in at the hotel, but there was such information and rumour flying around that I think I forgot to have a drink.' He paused, tasting his mouth. 'Yes, I must have done. This unfamiliar sensation is the taste of beerlessness. Never mind, I can make up for it later. You see, there's been an arrest.'

'Jim Daiches?' I said. This was terrible. I was going to have to come clean if Beth had not already done so on my behalf. But I refused to allow my apprehension to override my duties as a host. 'Help yourself to a beer, if your tongue's hanging out.'

'Not now, thanks. Jim, you may be pleased to hear, is back at home, without a stain on his character. It seems that they had another anonymous letter, pushed under the caravan door during the early hours of the morning, just like the others. According to Flora's boyfriend, they thought that it was just the same mixture of truths, half-truths and malicious irrelevancies as the other ones, but when they followed it up they found . . . that it wasn't.' Henry paused to enjoy our mystification.

It was a relief to know that Jim Daiches was off the hook. There was hope for me yet. 'Joe Little,' I said suddenly.

Henry looked at me, blank-faced. 'What put Joe into your head?' he asked.

'I woke up in the night. Or else I had a dream. But something reminded me that Joe bought another dummy-launcher off us not long ago. Then he came to me for two-two ammunition, just before Mrs Daiches was shot. He only used the cartridges as blanks and now he can't account for the bullets.'

'Why on earth would Joe Little want to kill Laura Daiches?' Isobel asked me. 'He's a Labrador man,' she added, as though that would remove any point of contact.

'I don't know. But . . . ' Suddenly my dream came back to me. 'I had a dream last night. It seemed quite reasonable at the time, but in the light of day it's ridiculous.' I found myself laughing. 'I dreamed that Joe was really breeding spaniels, but he was ashamed of them so he dyed them black and passed them off as Labradors.'

173

'That's really quite clever,' Beth said.

'Don't laugh at me,' I said. 'It's crazy. But I had a sudden picture in my mind of Joe drilling the rest of the way through the spigot of a launcher. It would explain why he needed another one.'

'So would the fact that he lost the one he'd been using,' Isobel said. 'He couldn't remember where he'd put it down while he attended to a dog which had slashed itself on barbed wire. I found it on The Moss yesterday and returned it to him. He said that he was grateful, because now he's got a spare one.'

Henry was openly chortling. 'According to our secret source – Flora's friend in the fuzz – a preliminary report on the bullet refers to rifling marks. A hole drilled through a dummy launcher wouldn't have rifling.'

'Ian West's airgun,' Isobel said positively, 'and a bullet out of Joe Little's jeep. Probably that bloody vet did it. She and Olive Cory had been making his life a misery over the valuation of Olive's blasted dog.'

'Or Andrew Williamson with his rifle,' I said.

Henry chuckled until he nearly choked. 'I'll tell you some more. The number and pitch of the rifling grooves suggested a well-known make of two-two adaptor,' he said. 'Following up a lead in the anonymous letter, the police found just such an adaptor under a pile of coal. They suspected a frame-up, but apparently the letter gave a lot of other details which all checked out. I don't know what those details were, but they've been rousting experts on show spaniels out of bed. And not always their own beds either.'

'Whose pile of coal?' Isobel wailed. 'Stop tormenting us!'

'Laurie Duffus's?' I suggested. 'She quarrelled with him once too often, so he taped the noise of himself hammering away and left the tape playing, to give himself an alibi while he slipped round to do the deed.'

Henry sobered and looked at me as though I were mad. 'If Laurie Duffus had an adaptor under his pile of coal – and anyway he's oil-fired – why would they have arrested Olive Cory?'

The silence seemed to hiss. Or perhaps it was the blood in my ears. Beth was impassive but Isobel looked as bemused as I was.

'Mrs Cory?' I said at last. 'That can't be right. You must mean Neill. Mrs Cory wouldn't know about adaptors. Or were they working together?'

'Neill seems to have been as surprised as anybody, and more so than most,' Henry said. 'Anyway, he was in the hotel, talking to me, when the murder must have happened. I think I'll have that beer after all.'

'But why would she kill her best friend and only witness?' I asked him.

He got up and fumbled with the cabinet where I kept the drink. I tried to catch Beth's eye but she seemed very interested in the overhead lampshade.

Henry sat down and took a long pull at his beer. 'That's better,' he said. 'I can recognise myself now. When did that woman ever need a good reason for anything? The police are satisfied as to the motive although they aren't saying much as yet. But I can tell you something else. Years and years ago when Jim Daiches and Neill shared that small shoot, they used to invite me to shoot with them now and again. Their wives came along, to beat and work the dogs. Olive could never get the hang of swinging a shotgun. But they had a cat in those days which wouldn't eat anything but rabbit, and not out of a tin. Olive got very clever at stalking rabbits with Neill's gun – an even older one than the gun he has now – with his adaptor in it. But the cat died, the girls decided that shooting was cruel and Neill traded his adaptor in against a newer gun. A single-barrel again – he said, I remember, that cartridges were expensive and he'd no desire to miss the same damn bird twice. God knows where she got an adaptor from. They aren't exactly common on the ground. But at least she'd know a little about how to use one. She'd have had no trouble getting her hands on

Neill's shotgun. He's never very fussy about locking it up, and he was in the hotel when she needed it.'

Silence fell again, but this time it was reflective rather than stunned.

'I could believe in Olive Cory as an anonymous letter writer,' Isobel said. 'But murder? Shooting followed by strangulation? They'll never get a jury to believe it of a woman.'

'She's confessed,' Henry said simply. 'She began by denying everything. Then she started throwing wild accusations around. She even claimed to be the writer of the other anonymous letters, as if that would somehow make the last one spurious and unreliable. She kept being caught up in contradictions until finally she lost her temper and blurted out the whole story in a sort of "See what happens to people who get in my way" manner.'

'Now, that I can believe,' Isobel said. 'That sounds exactly like her, to cut her own throat with the edge of her tongue.' The murmur of a car in the drive and some barking over the loudspeakers interrupted us. 'Oh Lord! They're here,' she said. 'Not the police,' she added kindly to me, seeing my reaction. 'Although some day you're going to tell me why you keep jumping out of your skin whenever they're mentioned. Ben's owners phoned, to ask how he was getting on. I suggested that they come and visit him. I know we don't usually like owners to visit but in the circumstances ... After all, they're spending money on him, so I think we owe them a chance to make their own decisions. Do you feel up to seeing them?'

'It's my job,' I said sadly. 'You'd better leave me alone with them. And, Beth, would you take Ben away until I call you?'

Isobel brought me up to date on Ben's condition. Her words were not comforting. 'And now I'd better get on with something useful,' she said. 'Henry, you can come and help.'

Henry finished his beer and followed her out at heel.

It was only a few days since I had seen the couple last, but when Isobel showed them in, the young woman – Mrs Sturges, Isobel had reminded me – seemed even more pregnant than before.

'Don't get up,' Mr Sturges said. He made sure that his wife was safely seated before lowering himself into the other wing-chair. 'I hear that you've been ill,' he said. 'And you look poorly. Should we be bothering you?'

'I'm on the mend,' I said. 'I reacted badly to a new treatment.'

'Mrs Kitts asked us to come in.' He hesitated and then rushed in with the question which was in both their minds. 'Have you managed to do anything with Ben?'

'If this wasn't something we both care too much about for joking,' I said, 'I'd ask you whether you want the good news or the bad news first. I've done a lot with Ben, but I have to tell you that there's a congenital reason why he'll never be the pet you're looking for.' I explained about retinal dysplasia. 'You can get other opinions by all means,' I said. 'We can put you in touch with a vet on the Eye Panel of the Royal College if you like. But my partner's a vet and she's very experienced at spotting early signs. She says that retinal detachment has already started. I didn't want you to see the progress he'd made until you knew about his condition. You see, there's a high probability that you'd end up with a blind or near-blind dog on your hands.'

Mrs Sturges began to lean forward but her pregnancy obstructed the movement. She was probably a plain young woman at ordinary times but the glow of pregnancy lent her a temporary charm. She sat back and met my eyes. 'It's not certain then?'

'Nothing about it is certain. It varies from one case to another. Isobel's opinion is that his sight will fail.' I was putting it bluntly, but that seemed kinder than leaving false hopes. 'You have a difficult decision to make,' I went on. 'I'll quite understand if you'd rather not see him again. But you'll realise that there would be little hope of finding another home for him.'

'We understand that,' Sturges said.

'I don't know where you got him from, but a reputable breeder would give you your money back or another dog.'

They conferred, in their silent way.

'Would he be all right with children?' Mrs Sturges asked.

'That might depend largely on yourselves,' I told her. 'He may have a year or two of acceptable vision. He'd know your first-born. Any late arrivals or visitors would have to be properly introduced. But they get very clever at managing without sight.'

'Like people,' Mrs Sturges said.

'Better than people, if they're given the chance. Your problem would come at holiday times – he'd never take to kennels. And he'd have great difficulty if you ever moved house.'

'We're settled where we are. I think we'd like to see him,' she said. Her husband nodded.

'Try not to show emotion,' I said. 'Don't move or speak until I tell you.'

I called to Beth. She came in with Ben walking tidily to heel, off the leash. He never glanced at the other occupants of the room but I saw his nostrils twitch. He checked when he sensed who was present but at a sharp word he came back to heel. I was mentally kicking myself. Ben's vision was already deteriorating and at least a part of his learning difficulty had been his inability to read the body language which often forms an important element in a command.

Beth walked him twice round the room. His eyes had found his owners and never left them. Beth stopped and Ben sat.

'Now call him,' I said. 'And make a movement. A dog's sight is much more sensitive to movement than to shapes.'

Mrs Sturges said, 'Come, Ben,' and lifted her hand. Ben looked up at Beth for approval and then walked gently forward and laid his head on his mistress's knee. It was a performance quite different from his usual impetuous bounce. I had put a lot of work in on Ben, but not enough to explain such a change. I can still only think that those sensitive instincts had drawn some message out of the change in our attitudes to him.

'It's amazing,' Mr Sturges said. 'We hoped that you could help, but we never expected so much. And to find, after all that, that he'll go blind . . . I'd like to keep him.'

'So would I,' said his wife. She looked at me.

'What would you do,' Sturges asked me, 'if he were yours?'

I remembered pinning Dr Harper down with a similar question. He had my sympathy now. 'If Ben were part of my stock in the kennels,' I said, 'I would put him down straight away. But if he were my personal dog I'd keep him, no matter what difficulties I might have to face.'

'It wouldn't be cruel?'

They were turning to me as if to a prophet, expecting answers which they could take as Gospel. It seemed very important that I should say the right things. 'That's a matter of opinion. If I ever lose my sight,' I said, 'I'll still put up a hell of a fight if somebody wants to put me out of what he believes to be my misery. A dog doesn't ask much. To be fed and loved and walked and allowed to sleep in comfort. To be part of a family and to know his place in it. And they depend much less on sight than we do. They live in a world of scent and hearing. The brain is smaller than ours and because the other senses take up more than their fair share of it only a tiny portion is available to process the signals from the eyes. They're colour-blind except at close range and, although they're quick to detect a movement, most of the unmoving world around them is probably only a greyish blur of unfocused shapes. For a dog, to go blind may be less than the loss of your hearing would be to you. But Ben will lose the early warning system which a dog gets from having vision sensitive to movement. You'd have to protect him from surprises.'

Mrs Sturges was rubbing Ben's head behind the ears. 'We'll keep him,' she said.

'But you're sure you know what you'd be taking on?'

'Not all of it,' she said. 'We'll find out as we go along. I think we owe him that much.'

'I'm glad,' I said. 'My first reaction was that if you didn't want him I'd keep him myself, but we're in business here. My partner would have kittens if I started to fill the kennels with liabilities. Now that we know what we're working towards, give me a week to polish him.' But I remembered that in a week I would be down in London for more blood tests. 'Make it a fortnight. Then I'll give you a lesson in how to keep him up to scratch and how to cope as his sight deteriorates. After that, you can take him . . . home.'

Beth showed them out. Ben looked after them longingly but seemed to accept that he must stay. I found that I was blinking rapidly. Poor Ben had found a breach in my emotional defences. And, I told myself, I was unusually vulnerable after my collapse. Pure sentimentality, of course.

When she returned, Beth leaned back against the door and made ashamed use of her handkerchief. 'I'm being stupid again, aren't I?' she said.

'Not stupid at all,' I said. 'I feel exactly the same. Come and sit down beside me for a minute.'

She sat down at the other end of the settee. I reached out and captured her hand. It was warm and dry and absolutely right. This was the first time that I could remember making more than accidental physical contact with her and, once she had got over the initial strangeness of it, I felt a current flowing.

'Now,' I said. 'It's time for a talk. I can guess what

you did. But before I get carried away on an orgasm of curiosity and apprehension, for God's sake tell me how and why.'

'I should be helping Isobel,' she said.

'I'm an invalid. You've got to humour me.'

# SIXTEEN

Beth looked at me for what seemed to be a long time. 'It might be better if I didn't tell you,' she said at last.

'Don't be— ' I broke off. Isobel had reminded me not to throw accusations of stupidity around. ' — over-cautious,' I amended. 'I can't go on evading questions for ever. One of these days, our friend the Sergeant, or somebody further up the ladder, will put me on the spot and if I don't know what you've done or said I may put my foot into it up to the neck.'

I waited.

'What do you think I did?' Beth asked quietly.

'Isobel says that you said something about two being able to play at that game.' I looked round. The door was closed and there was nobody at the window. Even so, I lowered my voice. 'My guess is that that makes you the writer of the last anonymous letter. I hope you were careful.'

'I wore Isobel's surgical gloves and took a piece of typing paper from the middle of the pack,' she said. 'And I used a ruler to make capital letters. Was that careful enough?'

'Quite enough, I should think. And you put the adaptor under the coal in Mrs Cory's shed? That's why you cleaned your shoes carefully when you got home?'

'Yes. That's where it had been. You said yourself that it was mucky. There was black dust on my duster after I wiped it. Well, I can tell coal-dust from household dust or gun-oil. I . . . I couldn't think of anything else to do. Poor Mr Daiches was in trouble which he didn't deserve and it was upsetting you and I couldn't let it go trailing on for ever and . . . and . . . '

She was still sniffling away. It seemed a lot of emotional reaction to be no more than the aftermath of Ben's salvation. I pulled gently on her hand and, as if absent-mindedly, she slid along the settee until I could put an arm around her. She leaned against me and her tension gradually drained out – through my arm and away to earth, it seemed.

'Calm down,' I said, 'and tell me all about it. But, for Heaven's sake, why Mrs Cory?'

'Because it was her. I was right, wasn't I?'

I put behind me any temptation to snap at her. Whatever she was, she was not stupid. Isobel had been right about that. Perhaps she had been right about the rest of it. 'If Henry has the story straight,' I said, 'you were absolutely on the ball.'

'I thought that it must have been Mr Cory at first,' she said, 'until I realised that he'd been in the pub at the time of the murder and again when Samson was poisoned. It had to be one of them. Nobody had been near us except the poisoner since Samson went into the isolation kennel, but when Mr Daiches came here he knew about it. And he said he hadn't seen anybody except the Corys.'

'He'd spoken to Mrs Spring on the phone,' I pointed out.

'That's why I offered to phone up and ask whether they could take the brood bitch and her pups. I asked Mrs Spring, sort of casually, whether she'd heard anything about gastro-enteritis and she said that she hadn't.'

I thought about it. The argument might be logical but it was hardly enough evidence to justify quite such drastic action. 'It could as easily have been Jim Daiches himself,' I said. 'He seems to have had the motive. And he often came home to lunch in mid-week if he was seeing clients. He could have borrowed my adaptor.'

'Yes, but at the time when Samson was poisoned he was

the one person who couldn't have gone wandering around without the police or somebody noticing. I mean, he was the husband of the murdered woman, the police caravan was next door, the police were in and out of the house and he'd stopped going outside. Anyway, he wasn't lying when he talked to us. I could tell. And there's another thing. He had a shotgun. Well, you'd know more about these things than I would, but how would you use a Coke bottle as a silencer on a double-barrel gun?'

It was a point which had not occurred to me and I felt a momentary pang of indignation that it took a chit of a girl to point out the obvious. 'With some difficulty,' I said, 'although the police must have thought that it could be done. Was that all you had to go on? It doesn't seem a lot of evidence to justify quite such drastic action.'

She shook her head so that her hair tickled my face. 'You can make any one thing sound silly,' she said reproachfully. 'But it was a whole lot of things coming together. Look at it this way. Suppose that one of us was in an accident or had a loss of memory. Suppose that it was me and you came to identify me and the police asked you how you knew it was me. How would you describe me?'

'Very pretty,' I said, 'with dark hair and looks about fifteen.'

'Really?' She thought about that for a long moment and squeezed my hand against her. 'Well, we can go into that later. If they asked me the same about you, I could only say that you were very thin and didn't look well but that you had an infectious smile when you cared to use it. Do you see what I mean?'

'You mean that it's not individual items that matter but how the whole thing comes together.'

'Sort of. You look at somebody, you notice and you know. What I was talking about earlier was what made me wonder about Mrs Cory. It was the whole picture coming together that made me sure. At first I couldn't think why she'd have done such a thing. And then when Mrs Kitts started talking about RD and Lucasta of Coneyshaw it all seemed to click together. Do you want me to go over it?'

'I think you'd better,' I said. I was beginning to have a vague idea of what she was talking about but I hoped that she would never realise just how vague it was.

Beth wriggled round into a more comfortable position, still hugging my hand against herself. 'I may not be very bright,' she said, 'but I never forget a dog. I knew that one of Mrs Cory's bitches was shot, but I'd seen her walking Culrosa since then. She and Dalgetty looked almost the same – they had the same sire in common. Their markings were identical. I couldn't point to any feature that you could point to as being special to one or the other. Yet there were little differences of expression and pace and the way they held their heads. I wasn't in any doubt. But Isobel Kitts said that Culrosa had been shot. Well, she remembers all about pedigrees and records, the way I remember the dogs themselves.

'I could only see one explanation. Because Culrosa was inclined to pass on retinal trouble, Mrs Cory must have been intending to phase her out and to bring on one of Dalgetty's pups to take her place. That would only be sensible. But Dalgetty was shot. And Mrs Cory's younger bitch was a full sister of Culrosa. Mr Cory's business hadn't been earning much lately, and there was going to be a lawsuit about the dead sheep and so on, so the money from breeding would be important, wouldn't it?'

'Yes, of course,' I said. One or more litters a year, each of up to eight or ten pups from a winning spaniel strain, would be worth real money. 'But Mrs Daiches was there. She'd have known which dog was shot.'

'Mrs Daiches never had eyes for anybody else's dogs. She'd accept whatever Mrs Cory told her. So what Mrs Cory did was to tell the Kennel Club and everybody else that Culrosa had been shot, and pass off her pups as Dalgetty's. Dalgetty had taken some prizes when she was younger and had produced some prizewinning pups. She was clear of congenital defects. Mrs Cory could go on raking in the money until she could buy or breed replacements.'

I gave a surprised whistle. I must have nearly deafened Beth, because she put up a finger and wiggled it in her ear.

'Breeders can sometimes be unscrupulous,' I said, 'but that takes the biscuit. And she'd get away with it . . . until RD showed up again. As in Ian West's young dog,' I remembered suddenly.

'Exactly,' Beth said. 'When she sold a puppy, she probably said a few soothing words about congenital defects but she wouldn't have put anything in writing. You know what they say about a verbal guarantee not being worth the paper it's written on? Well, my guess was that the woman visitor, the one Mr Daiches saw speaking to his wife and Mrs Cory, was one of the purchasers whose dogs were going blind. She was raising hell and insisting on her money back or something, and Mrs Daiches was backing her up. Mrs Cory probably disputed the diagnosis or tried to blame bad feeding or an accident, or else just told the woman to go and play in the traffic. And she may not have been the first one.'

Belatedly, I was catching up with her. 'And that gave Mrs Daiches the clue she needed to puzzle it out for herself,' I said. 'Whatever I've said about her blasted dogs, she wouldn't have stood for deliberately passing on a strain of RD. She may have been misguided but at least she cared. That was why she put off making any signed statement.'

'What do you think she'd have done about it?' Beth asked.

I wondered what I would have done in the circumstances. 'She'd certainly have told her old friend to stop breeding from Culrosa,' I said, 'and not to show any dogs until she'd put matters to rights. She probably told her to buy back every defective puppy. In fact, God knows what she'd told her to do, but whatever it was it would have rocked her rather precarious financial boat for her.'

'And hurt her pride,' Beth said. 'Mrs Cory may even have threatened her – Laurie Duffus heard Mrs Daiches' voice telling somebody not to come near her . . . "until this is settled".'

Another thought caught up with me. 'I'll bet that's what her row was about with the vet. A valuable bitch had been shot. But she'd need a valuation for insurance purposes. If she passed the corpse off as the less valuable bitch and the vet knew about the genetic defect, the vet's valuation would be low. Mrs Cory would be hoist with her own petard. She'd be fizzing mad.'

'She does have a rather low fizz threshold,' Beth said.

'And while she was wondering how she could dig herself out of the mire, it occurred to her that Mrs Daiches' death would not only remove the immediate threat but would make fresh breeding stock available to her.' It was really Beth's story to tell but I felt a compulsion to join in, just to show that I also was capable of reasoning. 'But Mrs Daiches, sensibly, wouldn't let her come within reach. Her husband's shotgun was available, but there would be no mistaking the slam of a twelve-bore. The neighbours would probably have come running. Then, when she came up here in search of dogfood or something, she found the shop unlocked. She recognised the adaptor. She had used Neill's one, years before. But what would she do for ammunition? Mine was all locked up.'

'Two-two ammunition wouldn't be difficult to come by,' Beth said. 'I mean, whatever the Firearms Act says, men carry it in their pockets, drop it around or leave it in dishes on hall tables.'

Out of her sight, I made a face. I had been guilty of all those sins. 'She couldn't count on something like that if she wanted cartridges suddenly and in a hurry,' I said.

She shook her head, tickling my nose with her hair again. 'But I thought – and you can tell me if I'm wrong – that if she'd seen the bullets in Joe Little's car and knew that she could take one or two of them, and then she spotted your adaptor when she found the shop open, it might occur to her to take one or two of the blanks for your dummy launcher. From what Mr Kitts said, she used to be quite familiar with all those things. If she put the adaptor into her husband's shotgun and pushed a bullet into the chamber of the adaptor and put a launcher blank up behind it . . . Would that work?' she asked anxiously.

'I should think it would work to perfection,' I said. 'Those blanks kick like hell and throw a half-pound dummy nearly a hundred yards. If that's what she used, no wonder she put a bullet right through Mrs Daiches.'

'Would it be noisy?'

'I think it might. But Neill Cory's single-barrel shotgun would take a plastic Coke-bottle for a silencer without much difficulty. From memory, the neck of one of those bottles is about the size of a twelve-bore barrel, give or take a little sticky tape. I don't know how quiet that would make it, but if Laurie Duffus was banging in nails at the time I don't suppose that anybody would notice. Hammering tends to be rhythmical and it would be easy to synchronise the shot with one of his hammer blows. The neighbours would be trying to close their ears to the hammering, so if they noticed anything they'd put it down to Laurie having produced an extra loud wallop or his hammer having skidded off the head of a nail.'

'That's pretty much what I was thinking.' Beth screwed her head round and looked at me from a few inches. Her lashes looked enormous. I thought that I had never realised before how much a brown eye could say. 'But then, if Mrs Daiches wasn't killed outright, why go into the garden and strangle her? Why not another bullet?'

I was ready for that one. 'Because,' I said, 'if you're not familiar with adaptors, you don't line up the extractor properly with the extractor in the gun.'

'That's the thing that pushes out the fired cartridge?'

'Right. So when you open the gun, the whole adaptor

tube comes up instead of the extractor just pushing up the empty cartridge case. She'd have to wait until she got home and under a light before she could puzzle it out and extract the fired case. What beats me is what all the dog-poisoning was about.'

'Let's look at it another way round,' Beth said. She settled back comfortably again. 'Mrs Cory thought about it and then decided to defy Mrs Daiches. Mrs D. realised that she'd have an awful job proving anything and even then she'd be risking an action for defamation or something and in the meantime a lot of damage could be done to the spaniel gene-pool and to the reputation of breeders in general. Well, she wasn't a woman who gave up easily. She put paid to that possibility by poisoning the bitch. She probably meant to kill both of them.

'And then, I suppose, she said something like, "That's stopped your little game for the moment. Now you can jolly well give those people back their money and start again with a clean blood line."

'That's what pushed Mrs Cory too far. The perfect time was in the dark that Friday evening, when Mrs Daiches came out to feed her dogs, with Mr Daiches away and Laurie hammering. Nobody was likely to see her crossing between the last two houses in the village, beyond the street lights. But once she'd done the murder, she had another problem to solve. A poisoned dog followed by a murder drew attention back to her; any fool might think about revenge and start putting two and two together. She used the anonymous letters to feed the police anything she thought might keep them busy and looking in all the wrong places. But then she must have thought that two poisonings, one before and one after the murder, would confuse the whole issue and make it look as if something quite different was going on. If the same poisoner had struck twice, it couldn't have been Mrs Daiches.

'I dare say that any dog would have done. But she saw us, and Henry, in the hotel, and you annoyed her. She must already have had her knife into you because putting back the adaptor and tipping off the police didn't seem to have worked. So she paid us another visit.'

'And the dogs didn't warn Isobel?'

'I hadn't finished,' Beth said severely. 'And you're forgetting the wrong-number phone call. You know what Mrs Cory always carried in that big handbag?'

'No idea,' I said.

'She made no secret of it. She took a pride in never missing a call from a customer. So she carried one of those cordless telephones around with her. She arrived up here. But the curtains were open and Mrs Kitts was working in this room and the loudspeakers were on. She waited for her chance. And then Mrs Kitts went out to look at Samson.'

'Isobel should lock the doors when she's on her own,' I said.

'But she never does. She won't admit it, but I think it's because she can imagine running away from an intruder and coming up against a locked door. Mrs Cory knew how our system works – you showed it to her when she said she was thinking about getting something similar, remember? But she never bothered. I think she was just being nosy.

'So, when she got her chance, when Mrs Kitts went out to look at Samson, Mrs Cory nipped into the house and switched off the speakers.

'Mrs Kitts came back. Mrs Cory went to do the job, found Samson in the isolation kennel and chucked the meat in. If any dogs barked she waited until they settled down again. Then she phoned our number. Isobel had to go through to the office to answer it and Mrs Cory came into the hall and switched the alarms on again.'

'I thought that you had to be quite near your own house to use those things,' I said doubtfully.

'It varies,' Beth said. 'My brother has one. Sometimes, especially after dark, he says he can make calls from miles away. Anyway, that's how I saw it.'

'So you left out my adaptor but told them all the rest?' It occurred to me that Beth had already made out a better case than some which result in convictions.

'That's right. I told them where the adaptor was and what the motive had been. I thought that they would get proper evidence more easily than we could. Are you going to say that I just made a lucky guess?'

'Feminine intuition,' I said.

'If that's what you want to call it. Will it be all right about the adaptor now?'

Beth sounded anxious. I felt the same way until I had thought it out. 'No problem,' I said at last. A load was being lifted off me, piece by piece. 'Mrs Cory will have told them that she got the adaptor from here, but that won't have come as a surprise to them. If I deny ever having had such a thing their case against her will be damaged. To get my evidence, they'll do a deal.'

'So you think that I did the right thing?'

I nearly told her that that was a bloody silly question but I caught myself in time. 'You did very well,' I said. 'Brilliantly. Much better than I could have done. You're what Joe called you – a clever little madam.'

She gave a little sigh of contentment and turned towards me. Our knees got in the way so she hooked hers over mine.

'You may as well come the rest of the way and sit in my lap,' I said.

'I don't want to squash you.'

'You won't.'

'Suppose Mrs Kitts comes in.'

'I rather think,' I said, 'that Henry and Isobel intend to avoid this room until we come out. If we ever do.'

She wriggled up until she was resting lightly on my knees and leaning against me, deliciously intimate, near and yet far. 'Are you really going to get better now?' Her tone left me in no doubt that we had reached what was, for her, a much more important topic than a mere murder between neighbours.

'So Dr Harper says. He also says that it'll be a long road to travel. There may be setbacks. Can you be patient?'

She sighed contentedly. Her bosom moved against me. 'I've been patient for a long time,' she said. 'But I always knew that it would come right some day. What's a little longer?'

Ben, waking up and feeling jealous, tried unsuccessfully to force his way between us. But neither of us had any intention of moving. Soon, he gave up and went back to the hearth-rug.